WHY THE WHALES CAME

Also by Michael Morpurgo

Arthur: High King of Britain
Escape From Shangri-La
Friend or Foe
The Ghost of Grania O'Malley
Kensuke's Kingdom
King of the Cloud Forests
Little Foxes
Long Way Home
Mr Nobody's Eyes
My Friend Walter
Twist of Gold
Waiting for Anya
War Horse
The War of Jenkins' Ear
The White Horse of Zennor

For younger readers

Conker
The Marble Crusher
The Nine Lives of Montezuma
The Sandman and the Turtles

Edited by Michael Morpurgo

Muck and Magic: Stories from the Countryside
More Muck and Magic

WHY THE WHALES CAME

MICHAEL MORPURGO

CHILDREN'S LAUREATE

EGMONT

To Mark, Linda,
Geoffrey and Stewart

First published in Great Britain in 1985
by William Heinemann Ltd
Reissued 2001 by Egmont Books Ltd
239 Kensington High Street, London W8 6SA

ISBN 0 7497 4693 9

10 9 8

A CIP catalogue record for this title is available from the British Library

Typeset by Avon DataSet Ltd, Bidford on Avon, Warwickshire
Printed and bound in Great Britain by Cox & Wyman Ltd, Reading, Berkshire

My thanks to Marion and Keith Bennett
and Leonard Jenkins of Bryher,
and also to Roy Cooper of Tresco,
for their help in the writing of this book.

CONTENTS

I was brought up on Bryher, one of the Isles of Scilly. You can find them on any map, a scattering of tiny islands kicked out into the Atlantic by the boot of England.

I was about ten years old when it all happened. It was April 1914.

Gracie Jenkins, 1985

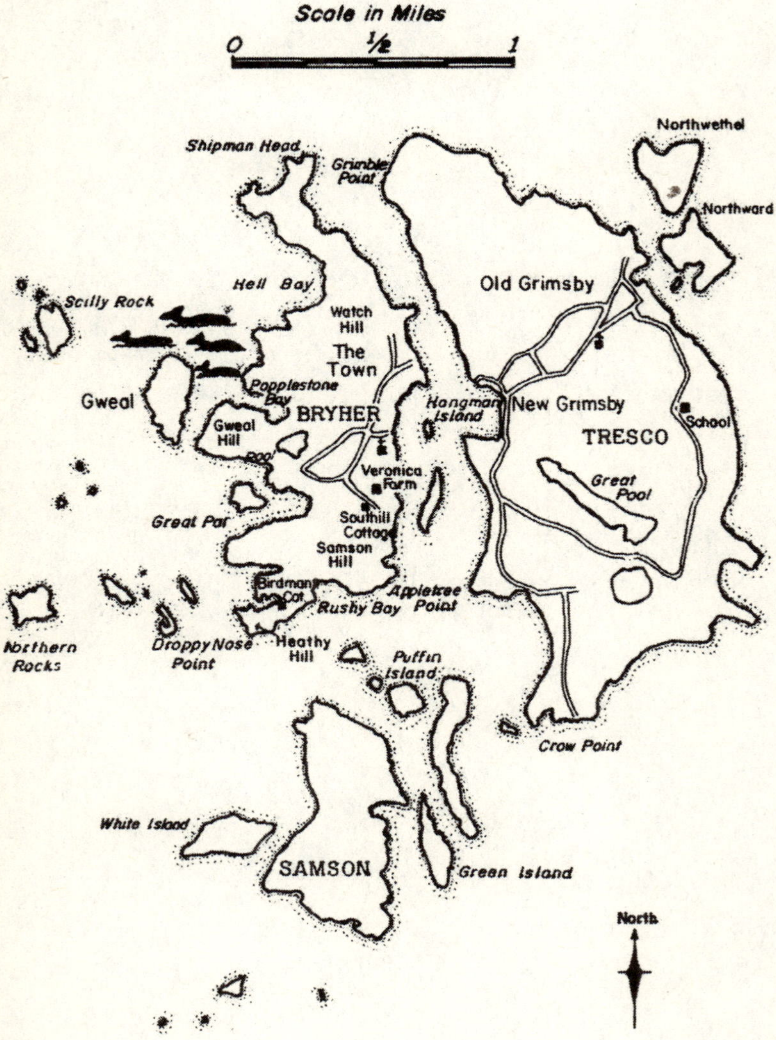

DETAIL FROM THE
ISLES OF SCILLY

1 Z.W.

'YOU KEEP AWAY FROM THE BIRDMAN, GRACIE,' MY father had warned me often enough. 'Keep well clear of him, you hear me now?' And we never would have gone anywhere near him, Daniel and I, had the swans not driven us away from the pool under Gweal Hill where we always went to sail our boats.

Daniel and I had built between us an entire fleet of little boats. Fourteen of them there were, each one light blue with a smart white stripe along the bulwarks. I remember well the warm spring day when we took them down to the pool in father's wheelbarrow. We had just the gentle, constant breeze we needed for a perfect day's sailing. We launched them one by one and then ran round to the far side of the pool to wait for them to come in. It was while we were waiting that a pair of swans came flying over, circled once and then landed in the middle of the pool, sending out great waves in their wake. Two of our boats keeled over and some were eventually washed back to the shore; but we had to wade in after the others to retrieve them. We tried shouting at the swans, we even threw sticks at them; but nothing we did would frighten them away. They simply ignored us, and cruised serenely around the pool, preening themselves. In the end it was we who had to leave, piling our boats into the wheelbarrow and trudging defeated and dejected home to tea.

For some days after that we tried to occupy our pool again, but the swans always seemed to be on the look-out for us and would come gliding towards us in a meaningful, menacing kind of way. They left us in no doubt that they did not want us there, and that they would not be prepared to share the pool with anyone.

So reluctantly we gave up and took our boats to nearby Popplestone Bay, but we found it was so windy there that even on the calmest of days our boats would be capsized or beached almost as soon as we pushed them out. And then one day the fastest boat in the fleet, *Cormorant* it was, was carried out to sea before we could do anything about it. The last we saw of her was the top of her yellow sail as she vanished in the trough of a wave. That was the last straw. After that we never sailed our boats from Popplestone Bay again. We were forced to look for somewhere else.

The beach on the sheltered coast of the island opposite Tresco would have been perfect, for the water was calmer here than anywhere else around the island, but there was always too much happening there. It was the hub of the island. Fishing boats were for ever coming in and going out, leaving great tidal waves behind them big enough to swamp our boats; and the children were often fishing off the quay or splashing through the shallows. Then there were Daniel's brothers and sisters, most of whom always seemed to be on that beach mending nets and lobster pots or painting boats. Of all of them, the one we most wanted to avoid was Big Tim, Daniel's eldest brother, and our chief tormentor; and he was always there. The one time we had tried to sail our boats there, he had come with his cronies and bombarded our fleet with stones. They had managed to break two of the masts, but to our great delight and their obvious disappointment, none of our boats was sunk. Even so, we did not want to risk it again. We had to find somewhere secret, somewhere where no one came and where the water was still enough for us to sail our boats. There was only one place left that we could go – Rushy Bay.

Rushy Bay was forbidden territory to us, along with most of the west coast of Bryher. The pool under Gweal Hill and the beach on Popplestones beyond was as far as any of us children were allowed to go in that direction. We never asked why, for we did not have to. We all knew well enough that the west coast of the island was dangerous, far too dangerous for children, whatever the weather. Mother and Father reminded me repeatedly about it, and they were right to do so. At Shipman's Head and Hell Bay there were black cliffs hundreds of feet high that rose sheer from the churning sea below. Here even on the calmest of days the waves could sweep you off the rocks and take you out to sea. I had been there often enough, but always with Father. We used to go there for firewood, collecting the driftwood off the rocky beaches and dragging it above the high-water mark to claim it for our own; or we would go for the seaweed, piling the cart high with it before going back home to dress the flower pieces or the potato fields. But I never went alone over to that side of the island, none of us ever did.

There was another more compelling reason though why we children were warned away from Rushy Bay and Droppy Nose Point and the west coast of the island, for this was the side of the island most frequented by the Birdman of Bryher. He was the only one who lived on that side of the island. He lived in the only house facing out over the west coast, a long, low thatched cottage on Heathy Hill overlooking Rushy Bay itself. No one ever went near him and no one ever spoke to him. Like all the other children on the island, Daniel and I had learnt from the cradle that the Birdman was to be avoided. Some said the Birdman was mad. Some said he was the devil himself, that he fed on dogs and cats, and that he would put spells and curses on you if you came too close.

The little I saw of the Birdman was enough to convince me that all the stories we heard about him must be true. He was more like an owl, a flitting creature of the dark, the dawn and the dusk. He would be seen outside only rarely in the daylight, perhaps out in his rowing boat around the island or sitting high on his cart; and even in the hottest summers he would always wear a black cape over his shoulders and a pointed black sou'wester on his head. From a distance you could hear him talking loudly to himself in a strange, unearthly monotone. Maybe it was not to himself that he talked but to the kittiwake that sat always on his shoulder or to the black jack donkey that pulled his cart wherever he went, or maybe it was to the great woolly dog with the greying muzzle that loped along beside him. The Birdman went everywhere barefoot, even in winter, a stooped black figure that lurched as he walked, one step always shorter than the other. And wherever he went he would be surrounded by a flock of screaming seagulls that circled and floated above him, tirelessly vigilant, almost as if they were protecting him. He rarely spoke to anyone, indeed he scarcely even looked at anyone.

Until now it had never even occurred to either Daniel or me to go alone into the forbidden parts of the island, nor to venture anywhere near the Birdman's cottage. After all, the island was over a mile long and half a mile across at its widest. We could roam free over more than half of it and that had always been enough. But Daniel and I had to have somewhere to sail our boats. It was all we lived for, and Rushy Bay was the only place we could do it. Even so I did not want to go there. For me it was far too close to the Birdman's cottage on Heathy Hill. It was Daniel who persuaded me – Daniel had a way with words, he always had.

'Look, Gracie, if we go up around the back of Samson Hill he won't see us coming, will he, not if we keep our heads down?'

'S'pose not,' I said. 'But he could if he was looking that way.'

'So what if he does anyway?' Daniel went on. 'We just run away don't we? He's an old man, Gracie, the oldest man on the island my Aunty Mildred says. And he limps, so he won't hardly be able to run after us and catch us, will he?'

'P'raps not, but . . .'

'Course he won't. There's nothing to be frightened of, Gracie. Anyway we'd have the whole of Rushy Bay to ourselves, nice calm sea and no Big Tim to bother us. No one's ever going to find us there.'

'But what if the Birdman does catch us, Daniel? I mean he's only got to touch us, that's what I heard.'

'Who told you that?'

'Big Tim. He said it was catching. Said the Birdman's only got to touch you and you'll catch it. Like measles, he said, like scarlet fever; and it's not the first time I've heard that either.'

'Catch what?' Daniel said. 'What do you mean?'

'Madness of course. It's catching, that's what Big Tim said anyway. Honest, you go loony, just like him if he touches you.'

'Tommyrot,' Daniel said. 'Course you won't. That's just Big Tim trying to frighten you. Don't you know him by now? He's full of stories, you know that. Honest, Gracie, you won't go mad or loony or anything else, I swear you won't. 'S not true anyway, and even if it was true he isn't going to get near enough to touch us, is he? Oh come on, Gracie, Rushy Bay's the only place left for us. We'll keep right to the far end of it, away from his cottage, so that if he does come we can see him coming and then we just run for it. All right?'

'What would Father say?' I asked weakly.

'Nothing, not if he doesn't know. And he won't, 'less you tell him of course. You wouldn't go and tell him would you?'

'Course not,' I said.

'Well that's all right then isn't it? Go tomorrow shall we?'

'S'pose so,' I said. But I was still not happy about it.

So we went the next day to Rushy Bay to sail our two fastest boats, *Shag* and *Turnstone*. It was a Sunday morning after church, I know that because I remember crouching in my pew beside mother that morning and asking God to protect me against the evil powers of the Birdman. When it came to the last words of the Our Father, 'And deliver us from Evil, Amen', I squeezed my eyes tight shut and prayed harder than ever before in my life.

As we crawled up through the heather on Samson Hill that morning I tried to turn back, but Daniel would not let me. He took my hand, smiled his sideways smile at me and said I would be all right because he was there and he would look after me. With Daniel and God on my side, I thought, my best friend on earth and my best friend in Heaven, surely nothing could go wrong. I was still trying to convince myself of this when we came over Samson Hill and saw the sand of Rushy Bay below us.

It was deserted just as Daniel had promised. We could

see the smoke rising from the two chimneys at either end of the Birdman's cottage and his two brown goats browsing in the heather beyond, but there was no sign of him anywhere. We sailed *Shag* and *Turnstone* until lunchtime. The wind was just right, blowing gently from east to west so that the boats fairly flew over the sea side by side. *Turnstone* was just that much faster – she always was – and I was worrying now only about the rigging on *Shag* which had somehow worked itself loose. I had already forgotten all about the Birdman.

When we went back for lunch we hid the boats in amongst the dunes; it would save us carrying them all the way home and all the way back again after lunch. But that afternoon when we returned to the spot we had left them, they were nowhere to be found. At first we thought we might both have been mistaken, that perhaps we had forgotten the exact place we had left them; but the more we searched the surer we were that they were gone and that someone must have taken them. I knew well enough who that someone must be.

I turned for home, calling to Daniel begging him to come with me. He was standing with his back to me on the top of the dunes, hands on hips, his shirt flapping around him, when suddenly he cried out and launched himself down over the dunes and out of sight. My mouth was dry with fear and I had a horrible dread in the pit of my stomach. But curiosity got the better of my fear and I followed him, even though he was running along the beach towards Heathy Hill, towards the Birdman's Cottage. All the while I called to him to come back, but he would not.

By the time I caught up with him he was crouching down on the sand just below the line of orange and yellow shells left by the high water. There were three boats lying at his feet in the soft white sand. I recognised them at once. There was *Shag, Turnstone* and beside them, *Cormorant.* Below them I could see two letters written out in orange shells: Z.W.

We both looked up expecting to see the Birdman standing over us, but there was no one. Smoke still rose from the chimneys in his cottage. The gulls ranged along the ridge of his thatch screeched at us unpleasantly. Then from the dunes close behind us a donkey brayed suddenly and noisily. That was enough even for Daniel. We picked up the boats and we ran; we did not stop running until we had reached the safety of Daniel's boatshed.

2 ISLAND OF GHOSTS

TEA WHEN I WAS A CHILD WAS ALWAYS FISH, FISH and potatoes; and that evening it was mullet, a great pink fish that stared up at me with glazed eyes from the platter. I had no appetite for it. All I could think of were those two letters in the sand on Rushy Bay. I had to know one way or the other – I had to be sure it was the Birdman.

I forced myself to eat the fish for I knew mother and father would suspect something if I did not, for mullet was known to be my favourite fish. We ate in silence, busying ourselves over the fish, so I had the whole meal to work out how best to ask them about the initials in the sand, without incriminating myself.

'Saw the Birdman today,' I said at last, as casually as I could.

'Hope you kept your distance,' said Father, pushing his plate away. 'With young Daniel Pender again were you?

Always with him aren't you?' And it was true I suppose. Daniel Pender and Gracie Jenkins were a pair, inseparable. We always had been. He lived just across the way from our front gate at Veronica Farm. Whatever we did, we did together. Father went on. 'Proper young scallywag his father says he is and I can believe it. You be sure he doesn't lead you into any trouble, my girl. Always looks like a big puppy that one with his arms and legs too long for the rest of him. Hair's always stood up on his head like he's just got out of bed. Proper scallywag he looks.'

'Looks aren't everything,' said mother quietly; and then she smiled and added, 'they can't be, can they, else how would I ever have come to pick you?'

'My beard, perhaps, Clemmie,' father laughed, and he stroked his beard and smoothed his moustache. He always called her 'Clemmie' when he was happy. It was 'Clem' when he was angry.

'You leave Daniel be,' said Mother. 'He's a clever boy, clever with his hands. You seen those boats he makes?'

'I help him,' I insisted. 'I paint them and I make the sails.'

'Been sailing them all day, I suppose,' said father. 'Out by the pool were you? That where you saw the Birdman?'

'Yes, Father,' I said; and then, 'About the Birdman, Father; everyone just calls him "The Birdman", but he must have a real name like other people, mustn't he?'

'Woodcock,' said father, sitting back in his chair and undoing a notch in his belt as he always did after a meal. 'Woodcock, that's what his mother was called anyway. You can see for yourself if you like – she's buried down in the churchyard somewhere. Last one to leave Samson they say she was, her and the boy. Starving they were by all accounts. Anyway, they came over to Bryher and built that cottage up there on Heathy Hill away from everyone else. The old woman died a few years after I was born. Must have been dead, oh thirty years or more now. The Birdman's lived on his own up there ever since. But you hear all sorts of things about his old mother. There's some will tell you she was a witch, and some say she was just plain mad. P'raps she was both, I don't know. Same with the Birdman; I don't know whether he's just mad or evil with it. Either way it's best to keep away from him. There's things I could tell you . . .'

'Don't go frightening her now with your stories,' said Mother. 'Anyway it's only rumours and tittle-tattle. I don't believe half of it. If anything goes wrong on this island they blame it on the Birdman. Lobsters aren't there to be caught – it's his fault. Blight in the potatoes – it's his fault. Anyone catches the fever – it's his fault. Dog goes missing – they say he's eaten it. Lot of old nonsense. He's just a bit simple, bit mad perhaps, that's all.'

'Simple my aunt,' Father said, getting up and going over to his chair by the stove. 'And what's more, it's not all tittle-tattle, Clemmie, not all of it. You know it's not.'

'There's no need to tell her any more,' said Mother. 'Long as she doesn't go anywhere near him, long as she keeps off Samson, that's all that matters. Don't you go filling her head with all those stories.'

'But they're not all stories, are they, Clemmie?

Remember what happened to Charlie Webber?'

'Charlie Webber? Who's he?' I asked.

'Never you mind about Charlie Webber,' said Mother; and she spoke firmly to Father.

'That's enough – you'll only frighten her.'

But Father ignored her. He leaned forward towards me in his chair, stuffing his pipe with tobacco. 'Charlie Webber was my best friend when I was a boy, Gracie. Got into all sorts of scrapes and capers together, Charlie and me. Nothing we wouldn't tell each other; and Charlie wouldn't ever have lied to me, not in a million years. He wasn't like that, was he, Clemmie?' But Mother wouldn't answer him. She walked away and busied herself at the sink. His voice dropped to a whisper now, almost as if he was afraid of being overheard. 'There's always been strange stories about Samson, Gracie. Course, people only half-believed them, but they've always steered clear of Samson all the same, just in case. But it was all on account of the Birdman and his mother that Samson became a place no one dared go near. They were the ones who put it about that there was a curse on the place. They were always warning everyone to keep off, so we did. They told everyone it was an island of ghosts, that whoever set foot on the place would bring the terrible curse of Samson down on his family. No one quite believed all that about ghosts and curses; but just the same everyone kept well clear of the place, everyone except Charlie.'

Father lit up his pipe and sat back in his chair which creaked underneath him as it always did whenever he moved. 'I never went over there, but Charlie did. It was a day I'll never forget, never, never – low tide, no water to speak of between Bryher and Samson. You could walk across. It was my idea, and not one I'm proud of, Gracie, I can tell you. It was me that dared Charlie Webber. I dared him to walk over to Samson. We were always daring each other to do silly things, that's just how we were; and Charlie Webber never could resist a dare. I stood on top of Samson Hill, and watched him running over the sands towards Samson, leaping the pools. It took him about ten minutes I suppose and there he was jumping up and down on the beach waving and shouting to me, when suddenly this man in a black sou'wester appeared out of the dunes behind him, came from nowhere. He began screaming at Charlie like some mad fiend and Charlie ran and ran and ran. He ran like a hare all the way back across the sand, stumbling and splashing through the shallows. By the time he reached me he was white with fear, Gracie, white with it I tell you. But that's not all of it. That very same night Charlie Webber's house was burnt to the ground. It's true, Gracie. Everyone managed to get out alive, but they never did find out what caused the fire; but Charlie knew all right, and I knew. Next day Charlie went down with the scarlet fever. I caught it after him and then near enough every child on the island got it. Aunty Mildred – you know Daniel's Aunty Mildred – she was just a baby at the time and she nearly died of it.'

'Did Charlie Webber die of it?' I asked.

'Now that's enough,' said Mother sharply. 'You've said enough.'

'Clem,' said Father, 'she's ten years old and she's not a baby any more. She's old enough to hear the rest of it.' He lit his pipe again, drawing on it deeply several times before he shook out the match. 'No, Gracie, Charlie didn't die, but he had to leave the island. His family was ruined, couldn't afford to rebuild the house. But before Charlie left for good he told me something I'll never forget. The day after the fire, Charlie was sitting on the quay when he felt someone behind him. He looked around and there was the Birdman. There was nowhere for Charlie to run to. He'd come, he said, to say sorry to Charlie, to explain to him that it wasn't his fault. There was nothing he could do once Charlie had set foot on Samson. He told Charlie that there was a curse on the island, that the ghosts of the dead haunted the place and could not rest, not until the guilt of Samson had been redeemed, whatever that meant. And when Charlie asked him why there was a curse on Samson, why the ghosts could not rest – this is what he told him. He was a little boy when it happened, younger than Charlie, he said. The people of Samson woke up one morning to find a ship run aground on a sandbank off Samson. Like a ghost ship it was on a flat calm sea. No fog, no wind, no reason for it to be there. They rowed out and hailed it, but no one answered; so they clambered on board. There was no one there. The ship was deserted. Well you don't look a gift horse in the mouth, do you? Every man on Samson, sixteen of them there were in all he said – every one of them was on that ship when it refloated at high tide. They sailed it off to Penzance to claim the salvage money, but they never got there. The ship foundered on the Wolf Rock, off Land's End, went down in broad daylight, mind you; gentle breeze, no fog. Every man on board was lost. The Birdman's own father went down on that ship, Gracie.'

'It's a horrible story,' said Mother, 'horrible. Every time I hear it it makes me shiver.'

'True nonetheless, Clemmie,' father said. 'And that wasn't the last of it. It seems things went from bad to worse on Samson after that. With no men left to go fishing or to work up the fields, the women and children soon began to go hungry. All they had to eat was limpets. The Birdman told Charlie that they even had to eat the dogs. It's true, Gracie, that's what Charlie told me. Then with the hunger came the fever, and the old folk and the babies began to die. So they left. One by one the families left the island until the Birdman and his mother were alone on Samson.'

Father drew on his pipe again and found it had gone out – his pipe was always going out. 'And I believe every word Charlie told me, Gracie. I don't pretend to understand the whys and wherefores; and I tell you straight, I don't know if it's him that's cursed or Samson. All I do know is that it's better to keep away from the both of them – that's for sure. So you keep well clear of him, you hear me now?'

I sat silent for some time lost in father's story, my head full of questions. 'So he can put spells and curses on people like they say he can?' I asked.

'Maybe,' said father, tapping his pipe out on the side of the stove. And I shivered as I thought of how close we had been to his cottage that day, and how he must have been watching us on Rushy Bay. Then there were those letters in the sand. Perhaps they were initials, but perhaps they were part of some spell. I wanted to be sure.

'What about his first name, Father?' I asked. 'Do you know his first name?' But immediately I regretted it for I felt Mother looking at me. I was being over inquisitive, too interested; and she was suspicious.

'Why all these sudden questions about the Birdman, Gracie?' she asked. 'You've never shown any interest in him before.'

'Just saw him today, like I said. Just wondered, that's all. Daniel and me, we just wondered about him.'

Mother came over and stood in front of me. She took my chin in her hand and pulled it up so that I had to look her in the eyes. She always did this when she thought I'd been up to some mischief and she wanted to get the truth out of me. 'You haven't been speaking to him, have you Gracie? You haven't been over on Heathy Hill, have you? You know you're not supposed to go there, don't you?'

'No, Mother, course I haven't, honest I haven't.' It was just as well I did not have to lie, for Mother would have known. Father I could deceive any time I wanted, but Mother knew me far too well. She looked down at me out of tired kind eyes, a knowing smile on her lips, so knowing that I had to look away.

'You leave him to his birds, Gracie,' father said. 'You keep well away like I said. Promise me now. You be a good girl and stay away.'

'I promise,' I said. 'I'll stay away.'

And so I did, for a day or so at least. It took only that long for Daniel to persuade me to go with him back to Rushy Bay, that we had been silly to run away in the first place just because we'd heard a donkey braying. I told him everything Father had told me about the Birdman and Samson and Charlie Webber. He listened, but I could see he didn't really believe any of it. He said he had heard something about the fire before, and that it didn't matter anyway because we weren't going to Samson like Charlie Webber did. We were only going to Rushy Bay. And the Birdman might be a bit loony, but what did that matter? He just wanted to make friends, that was all. Why else would he give us back our boat? Why else would he be leaving messages for us in the sand? We didn't have to go anywhere near him, did we? Perhaps I agreed to go with Daniel because I was half convinced by his arguments, or perhaps I was inquisitive.

When I crawled up over Samson Hill with Daniel that next day I kept flat on my stomach in the heather until I was sure the Birdman was not down there on Rushy Bay waiting for us.

The Birdman was not waiting for us, but something else was. Lying on its side in the sand in almost the same spot we had found our boats the day before was a bird, a cormorant. At first we thought it had been washed up dead, for it lay amongst the flotsam at the high water mark. As we approached I could see it was small even for a young bird, and that the feathers were not oily black as they should have been. I thought it must have been blown off the rocks before it could fly.

Suddenly Daniel caught my arm and pointed further along the beach. A trail of footprints led right to where the cormorant lay and away again. At that moment I would have panicked and run as I had done before, but this time Daniel's hand was firm on my arm and he led me forward. In the sand above the cormorant, written out in orange shells were the letters I now expected to find: 'Z.W.' It was not until we were down on our knees in the sand beside it that I realized the cormorant's feathers were not stirred by the breeze as they ought to have been, that it was in fact made of wood. Then we noticed the shells. Only a few feet away the shells along the tide-mark had been rearranged to read: 'Stay and play. Your beach as much as mine.'

We scanned the dunes above us for any sign of the black sou'wester amongst the reeds, but all we could see of the Birdman were his gulls still lined up on the thatch of his cottage watching us. Thin wisps of smoke rose from the chimney pots at each end of the cottage only to be whipped away at once and dissipated by the wind. Daniel reached out and picked up the cormorant. The base of it was carved out as a rock, covered with limpets and barnacles, and the cormorant stood on his great webbed feet, head slightly lifted, almost indignant. He was leaning forward as if balancing himself against the wind. All his feathers were so finely crafted that I expected them to be soft to the touch. Daniel set the bird down in the wet sand facing out over the water to Samson and sat back on his ankles.

'You ever seen anything like it?' he said stroking the crown of the bird's head. 'Looks as if he could lift off and fly, doesn't he?'

'D'you think the Birdman's watching us?' I whispered.

' 'Spect so. Don't mind if he is. Look at this, Gracie. The man who made this isn't a madman; he just can't be. And he gave us back our boat, didn't he? It's like I told you, Gracie, he's trying to make friends with us. He likes us being here. I'm going to stay and sail our boats, Gracie just like he said we could, and what's more I'm going to say thank you to him.'

'Well I'm not going anywhere near that cottage,' I said, suddenly cold with fear at the very thought of it. 'Not in a million years.'

'We don't need to, Gracie,' he said. 'Look.' And he wrote in shells beside the Birdman's message: 'Thanks. Daniel and Grace.'

'No,' I shouted as soon as I saw my name in the sand. 'You can't, you can't! He'll know who we are if you do that, he'll come after us and put his curses on us.' And I lifted my foot and kicked the sand all over Daniel's writing until I had obliterated every last letter. I was crying in spite of myself. 'Father says he puts spells on people. We mustn't talk to him. We're not supposed to.'

Daniel looked up at me and I could see from the look in his eyes that he was disappointed in me. 'But we're not going to talk to him, are we?' he said. 'Look, Gracie, it stands to reason. If the Birdman had wanted to put a spell on us he could have done it already, couldn't he? Well he could, couldn't he?' I would not answer him because I hated to be wrong, and I knew well enough in my heart that I was. In my shame and fury I kicked the cormorant over on its side and ran off up the beach towards Samson Hill. Daniel called after me to come back and all my rage at my own humiliating fear burst from me.

'If you're so brave, Daniel Pender,' I screamed at him, 'then you can sign your silly name; but I'm not coming here again, never, d'you hear me? Never. You can keep your silly boats and your silly cormorant for all I care. I don't want it and I don't want ever . . .', and I would have gone on to say every hurtful thing I could think of, had I not caught sight of the Birdman's dog plodding purposefully along the beach behind Daniel, his tongue lolling out of his mouth. I tried to call out to Daniel to warn him but my voice would not speak as it should, so I just pointed and ran back down over the sand to warn him.

The dog paid us no attention but went straight to where the cormorant lay and sniffed it. Then, arranging his jaws with care around it, he picked it up and came and sat tidily at our feet looking very pleased with himself, his tail swishing the sand behind him.

The dog seemed to have no eyes, for they were covered by a curtain of matted black ringlets. 'He's giving it to you,' I said. 'He wants you to take it.'

'For us is it?' Daniel asked the dog and he took the cormorant out of its mouth. 'Did he send you then, did the Birdman send you?' And the dog licked his lips and shook the sand out of his mouth. Daniel patted him and parted the hair over his face to reveal two shining black eyes. 'How can you see through all this lot?' he said.

And then the dog pricked up his ears, stood up and

looked around towards the cottage. He stopped panting for a moment and listened. Before we knew it he was bounding away over the sand and had vanished into the dunes. Neither of us had heard a whistle, but neither of us had any doubt at all that he had been called back.

'Must have been watching us,' I said. 'He must have seen me kick it over, mustn't he?'

Daniel brushed the sand off the cormorant's head. 'See, I told you, Gracie, didn't I? He just wants to be friendly, that's all.' And he dropped to his knees in the sand. 'Come on. We've got to thank him, haven't we?'

We never spoke a word after that but knelt in the sand together and collected all the shells we were going to need. Then I wrote out in orange shells: 'Thanks for the cormorant.' And both of us signed our names in shells underneath.

We stayed all day sailing our boats on Rushy Bay and even when Daniel suggested the sea was getting too rough I insisted we stayed on, just to prove to myself, to him and to the Birdman that I was no longer frightened. True, I did keep my eye on Heathy Hill, but now I was almost hoping the Birdman would come down to the beach with his dog. He did not come however, and my new-found courage was not put to the test, not yet anyway. As we left the beach Daniel cupped his hands to his mouth and called out, 'Goodbye', in the direction of the cottage, and I waved with him because I felt sure that the Birdman would be watching us.

Back in Daniel's boatshed that evening we stood by his workbench and examined the cormorant closely. 'One day, Gracie,' he said, 'one day, I'm going to be able to make something like that.'

'What happens if someone finds it?' I asked. 'What are we going to say?'

'Just tell them I made it,' he said laughing. 'But they may not believe us, so better if they don't find it. I haven't got a room of my own to hide it and I haven't got anywhere to put anything, not anywhere private anyway. You got a room of your own, Gracie, you keep it. It'll be safer with you. If Father finds it, he'll only want to know where it comes from and Big Tim will torture me till I tell him.' And he handed the cormorant carefully to me. I already knew where I would hide it – I was only worried about how I was going to get it there without being discovered.

'I've been thinking, Gracie,' Daniel said. 'He gave us this cormorant to show us he was friendly, didn't he? So we've got to do the same, haven't we? We've got to give him something back so's he knows we want to be friends as well. I've been thinking. D'you think he'd like it if we made him one of our boats?'

'Could call her *Woodcock*, couldn't we?' I said. 'We've got to name it after a bird, like all the others are. Woodcock's a kind of bird, isn't it?'

'Never seen one,' said Daniel, 'but I think it is.'

And so I went home that evening with the Birdman's cormorant stuffed inside my blouse. Mother paid me no attention as I came in; she was busy over the stove and I reached the safety of my room without her even seeing me.

We built *Woodcock* together that spring, but it was nearly summer before she was ready for launching. We had never taken so much trouble over a boat as we did with *Woodcock*. Nothing was ever right until it was perfect. We took her to Rushy Bay for her trials and pushed her out towards Samson Island. She danced out over the waves, her sail catching the wind and leaning her over so that she sped out to sea. I think she might have gone all the way to Samson had we not waded waist high into the sea after her and brought her back. She was quite magnificent with her shiny blue hull, her white stripe and her brick-red sail. Daniel was satisfied. So we left her, beached well above the high-water mark; and we left too a long shell message for the Birdman in the sand. It read: 'We name this boat *Woodcock*. May God bless her and all who sail her'; and we signed it, 'Daniel and Grace'.

We waited until sundown in the purple humming heather on Samson Hill to see if the Birdman would come for it, but he never came. We could not stay any longer for mother always liked me to be home before dark. But first thing the next morning we went back to Rushy Bay and found the boat gone. In its place there was this message: 'Thanks. Beautiful.' And underneath, 'Zachariah Woodcock.'

3 MESSAGES IN THE SAND

I NEVER MUCH LIKED GOING TO SCHOOL. IT WAS A nuisance for it took me away from home and from everything I wanted to be doing. But that summer it was more than a nuisance, it was an intrusion into our secret life on Rushy Bay and I resented it more than ever. I feigned sickness successfully on a few occasions, until Mother discovered that Daniel always seemed to be ill on the same day I was and put a stop to it. Sometimes, though not very often for Mother would have suspected me, I was able to persuade Father he could not do without me on the boat and I managed to stay off school that way. I knew we would only be out lobster fishing for the morning, so Daniel and I could spend the afternoon down on Rushy Bay. Father was never that hard to persuade because he liked the company and it did help to have me handling the boat whilst he set or hauled the lobster pots, particularly when there was a heavy swell out around the Northern Rocks.

It was always a great deal easier for Daniel to stay away from school because no one much cared in his house whether he was at school or not, and his father was only too pleased to have an extra pair of hands in the boatshed. Whatever happened though we always went to school together or stayed away together. It was not a formal pact between us, there was never any need for that – it was just an understanding.

School was across the water on Tresco. About fifteen of us went across on the boat each day from Bryher and we often had to get out and push the boat when it became stuck fast on the sandbanks at low tide. All day at my desk I longed for lessons to be over so that I could get back to Rushy Bay. It was hardly surprising therefore that my teacher, Mr Angus Wellbeloved, was for ever reprimanding me for lack of attention. Mr Wellbeloved, or 'Welly Belly' as we called him, grew a crop of long white hairs out of his ears which he always twiddled to a point whenever he was reading to us, and his wiry eyebrows joined in the middle of his nose and hung around his eyes like a misplaced moustache. From an early age Mr Wellbeloved had condemned me as 'unladylike', 'untidy' and 'unteachable', mostly because I could never master my arithmetic. For Mr Wellbeloved, arithmetic was the yardstick by which he judged character. Sums or anything to do with figures had always induced in me a kind of panic. I raged then against their peculiar logic. I could never understand them and I cannot to this day.

Only Daniel made it all bearable. We sat side by side

and survived school together. He did not care for school or for Mr Wellbeloved any more than I did, but he was clever enough to succeed at his sums and was therefore the apple of Mr Wellbeloved's eye. I copied just enough of his sums to get by and in return he copied my spellings whenever he needed to. I was a genius at spelling and proud of it. So with Daniel beside me I made an adequate pupil, just satisfactory enough to avoid being kept in for detentions, and that was all that mattered.

I may not have liked Mr Wellbeloved – few of us did – but it has to be said that it was Mr Wellbeloved who warned us early that summer that there would be a war with Germany before very long. I asked father about it and he told me it was all nonsense, and that anyway it did not much matter whether there was a war or not because no war could ever touch us on Bryher. I did notice that mother pursed her lips at this and kept silent, a sure sign that she did not share his optimism.

But even when school was finished for the day, Daniel and I were not free to go at once to Rushy Bay, for he was always needed to sweep up in his father's boatshed; and father might well send me out to fish for wrasse for lobster bait, or there were always lobster pots to be mended. Sometimes it could be almost evening before we were able at last to set off together. Even so, every day without fail we managed to get to Rushy Bay, not so much now to sail our boats, although we did if the wind was right, but rather to see if the Birdman had left another message for us in the sand.

Some days, to our intense disappointment, there

would be nothing there but a jumble of seaweed and flotsam. On most days though we would reach the top of Samson Hill and see the Birdman's dog waiting for us on the beach below. Whenever he was there we knew we would find a shell message in the sand beside him, or the remains of one anyway. Often he would be sitting so close to the message that by the time we got there his ever-wagging tail had scattered the shells far and wide, leaving us the problem of trying to make some sense out of the few surviving but scarcely decipherable letters. And leading to and from the message we would find the Birdman's distinctive footprints, the right foot broad and heavy, the left just half a footprint, five toes and the ball of the foot. It was always this left foot which dragged a continuous furrow through the sand from one print to the next.

Our exchange of shell messages became like a long drawn-out conversation. The messages took a long time to write out, so we kept them as short as possible. We tried to discover all we could about the Birdman, but by the end of the summer we still knew very little about him. We did manage to find out that he was exactly eighty years old, that the birds on the island came to him because he fed them, because they knew he liked them and because they knew he would never harm them. We learned he had been carving birds as long as he could remember, that his father had taught him. It kept his fingers from going stiff like the rest of him, and it made him feel like God because he could make any creature he wanted. All he needed was the wood, and there was plenty of that washed up on the beaches. That was all he would tell us about himself. He would simply ignore many of the questions we left behind for him; either that or the dog had wagged them out and ruined them before the Birdman could read them. We were fairly sure though that he was answering only those questions he wanted to answer.

He seemed quite happy however to tell us about his animals, so that we came to know a great deal more about them than we did about him. The donkey was called Friend, he told us. He had bad feet and a bad temper, mostly because he was old. Friend lived only for carrots which the Birdman grew exclusively for him in the garden. Just to look at him, the Birdman wrote, was to know that there was someone worse off than oneself. And he told us a lot about his dog, Prince, about how he had found him washed up in Hell Bay one day. 'Been with me a long time now,' he wrote. 'Don't know what I'd do without him.'

As the weeks passed, the pattern of questions and answers between us changed. It became clear he wanted to ask questions but not to answer them. At first he wanted to know everything about us, all about our families. He wanted to know how old they all were, what they looked like, where they lived and what they did. 'Father builds boats.' Daniel wrote one day.

'What kind of boats?'

'Gigs. Luggers. Anything.'

'Building one now?'

'Fishing lugger – 14ft.'

'Flower crop good this year?'

'Fair.'

'Potatoes? Any blight?'

'Late crop. No blight.'

And when the messages were longer the Birdman used bits of wood, even seaweed, to make his letters. But he always signed them 'Z.W.' in orange shells.

His appetite for news became more and more insatiable. For Daniel and me it was like having to describe the world to a blind man. He wanted to know everything people said, everything they did. It was after we had told him about Big Tim, about how much we hated him, that he first began to talk to us through his messages rather than simply to ask more questions. 'Never hate anyone,' he wrote. 'Hate eats away at your soul.' And when one evening we wrote that Mr Wellbeloved thought there would soon be a war with Germany we found his reply the next morning. It read simply: 'I am sad today.'

There was no time to build boats any more now for Daniel was busy with his first puffin carving. He had originally meant it to be a standing shag drying its wings, but no matter how hard he tried he could not get the head quite right, so he cut off the wings in disgust and reduced it to a rather bulbous-looking puffin that seemed to me more like an owl, but I did not dare say so. As it turned out I did not need to, for he soon discarded it and began another.

It was hot that August of 1914, hotter than any summer I have known since. The sand on Rushy Bay was too hot even to stand on by midday, so we had to retreat to the shelter of the dunes. Here Daniel would sit cross-legged in the sand whittling away at his new puffin, and I would brush out Prince's matted fur and pick the burrs out of the hair behind his ears while he lay panting beside me in the heat. When the sand had cooled in the late afternoon Prince would come with us down to the sea and cavort clumsily in the waves. He would swim out towards Samson for the sticks we threw for him and then lie beside us on the beach as we composed and wrote out our message in the sand for his master. But when we left for home at the end of the day he never once attempted to follow us. From the top of Samson Hill we would see him sitting alone on the beach still watching us, or trotting away up through the dunes back to the Birdman's cottage.

From time to time we did catch sight of the Birdman himself, but always at a distance. We would see him emerging from his cottage door at dusk to feed the chickens or milk the goats, or we might catch a glimpse of his boat bobbing up and down as he rowed out towards Samson. In the early evening sometimes we might see him setting off with his donkey and cart, up towards Hell Bay, Prince following along behind; but the closest we ever came to actually meeting him was one day when that summer was almost over.

We had left the beach later than usual that evening and were on our way back over Samson Hill when we saw him rowing out around Droppy Nose Point and into Rushy Bay itself. Above him flew his usual escort of shrieking, wheeling gulls. Prince was sitting where we had left him on the beach below. We shouted and waved but the Birdman had his back to us and never turned round. We felt sure he must be able to hear us for we heard his whistle clearly and saw Prince bounding down the beach and into the water. He paddled out through the sea towards the boat, his small black head rising and falling with the waves. We watched as the Birdman shipped his oars, leant down over the side and bundled him up into the boat. We saw Prince shake himself and heard the Birdman laugh and begin to talk as he took up the oars again. Prince stood up like a figurehead in the bow of the boat as it moved slowly out towards Samson, the flock of gulls circling above. All the while we could hear snatches of the Birdman's voice from across the water. He was too far away for us to hear what he was saying but we listened all the same, straining to pick up the sense of it over the sound of the surf.

'What d'you think he goes over to Samson for?' said Daniel. 'Nothing there 'cept empty houses and sand.'

'P'raps he goes fishing over there,' I said.

'He doesn't fish,' said Daniel. 'I've never seen him fishing, have you? And it's strange, Gracie, you only ever see him out in his boat in bad weather. Doesn't seem to bother him. You noticed that? I've seen him out in gales before now. He'll go out in any weather. Funny that, don't you think?'

I looked over towards where Samson lay brooding darkly under gathering storm clouds. About it the sea, blood-red with the evening sun, surged and heaved. 'Island of ghosts,' I said. 'Don't care what you say, Daniel, I tell you there's ghosts on Samson just like father said there was. You only got to look at it. It's cursed, Daniel, I can tell it is.'

'Don't believe in ghosts,' said Daniel dismissively, and he turned away. 'And I don't believe in curses either.'

'Well I do,' I snapped, suddenly angry at him, and we walked on down through the heather in silence.

The first few drops of rain were so huge and heavy that they hurt the top of my head. We began to run. The rain pounded us all the way home, stinging our eyes and ears. By the time we got there we were soaked through and dripping from our noses and chins. The houses all round were dark and quiet, unusually so. Only one light glowed at our kitchen window. 'Strange,' said Daniel, 'there's no lamps lit in my house. Everyone's out by the look of it. No one about, is there? Can't think where they could all be. Can't see anyone in the boatshed either. Can I come in with you, Gracie, till they get back?'

I knew full well how much Daniel hated to be alone in the dark. He was brave about everything else except the dark, and that always made me feel good because the dark had never bothered me. We shook ourselves in the porch and went in together.

Mother was sitting in the kitchen, her chair rocking back and forth. The lamp was on the table beside her and her sewing lay in her lap. I expected a wigging from her for being out after dark but she looked up vacantly at us as we came in and seemed neither annoyed nor surprised that we were late.

'Well,' she said, a weak smile on her face. 'You're back.' And then, 'I'm afraid your Mr Wellbeloved was right after all, Gracie. I thought he might be you know. I didn't want to believe him, no one did, your father least of all; but he's an educated man, Mr Wellbeloved, he could see it coming.'

'Right about what, Mother?' I asked. 'What's happened?'

'Where is everyone?' Daniel asked. 'Can't find anyone at home.'

'They've all gone to a meeting in the church, Daniel. Father's gone too, Gracie. They called an island meeting as soon as they heard the news this afternoon.'

'It's the war, isn't it?' Daniel said. 'They've started the war, Gracie, like old Welly Belly said they would.' And mother nodded and lowered her head.

There was such a storm that first night of the war, a violent thunderstorm that flashed and rolled around the island as if it wanted to uproot it from the sea. The wind moaned and howled horribly through the house. White sheet lightning turned the night to day outside my window heralding each new rumbling crescendo of thunder.

I was still awake when Father came in later that night. I heard him talking on and on about the war and about how the Germans had it coming to them, about how they had bitten off more than they could chew, about how we were better sailors than they were because we were an island race with the sea bred into us. It would not take long to finish them, he said, and we were going to do our bit on Bryher. By day there would always be someone on the look-out for submarines up on Watch Hill; and by night there were to be no lights showing on the island, all curtains were to be drawn and the island blacked out completely. All the while I never heard Mother speak a word. But what kept me awake had nothing to do either with the war or the storm, for I had no idea then what a war really was. I thought the war like the storm would pass soon enough. I lay there all that night thinking only of the Birdman and Prince out in the tiny boat, and I prayed and prayed that they had not been caught out in the open sea when the storm broke.

4 THE BIRDMAN

DANIEL WAS WAITING OUTSIDE MY FRONT GATE early the next morning. He too had scarcely slept for worrying about the Birdman and Prince. 'I just hope he reached Samson and stayed the night there, that's all,' he said. 'He wouldn't have had time to get there and back. I know he wouldn't. P'raps it's all right though. After all he must know that stretch of water better than anyone. Come on, Gracie, let's hurry.' And we ran all the way up over Samson Hill and only stopped for breath when we could see Rushy Bay below us.

By now the force of the storm was spent and the wind had died, but the sea was still seething and angry. The waves rolled into the bay from Samson, gathering and rearing as they neared the shore before they curled over to hurl themselves into the hissing sand. The beach was empty. There was no Prince waiting for us and we could find no message in the sand. We could see the storm had thrown up a line of debris high under the dunes and must certainly have washed away any message the Birdman might have left behind for us. Nonetheless we had to be sure, so we searched the thin strip of dry clear sand under the dunes, just in case. That was how we came across the oar, half-hidden under a tangle of seaweed.

Daniel helped me to pull it clear and we carried it up onto the clean sand. 'Could be anyone's, couldn't it?' I said, but Daniel said nothing. We scoured the beach together, picking over the flotsam, hoping against hope we would not come across what we were now both expecting to find, the shattered and torn timbers of the Birdman's boat. We found wood enough and plenty but it was white, wave-washed and smooth. There was no trace either of his boat nor of the other oar. I was relieved and heartened enough by this time to imagine that all must be well, that we had indeed found an oar from someone else's boat, but Daniel insisted that we should go over to Great Par, the beach on the other side of Heathy Hill where we knew the Birdman always kept his boat.

'If they are back safely like you say they are,' said Daniel, 'then the boat will be there, won't it, and we won't have to worry any more, will we?'

We left the oar lying on top of the dunes and made our way through the reeds towards Great Par. We walked on together in silence, and all the while I dreaded we might find nothing there, that my worst fears would be realised. As we came to the top of each dune more and more of the beach came into view, and still there was no boat to be seen. We were passing just below the Birdman's cottage when Daniel stopped suddenly and caught my arm. 'There's no smoke, Gracie,' he said, his voice hushed to a whisper. 'Look, can't you see, there's no smoke coming out of the chimneys. There's always been smoke before, I know there has. And there's no gulls either, there's no gulls on the roof.' I looked up at the cottage which was almost camouflaged against the background of heather on Heathy Hill and I could see Daniel was right, that the place was indeed deserted. The front door banged in the wind and no one came to shut it. A corner of the thatch had been ripped away by the storm and lay strewn around the potato field below the house. There was no sign of life on the hill except for the Birdman's two goats that clambered amongst the rocks at the top of Droppy Nose Point. Then a solitary gull flew over and hung on the wind above the cottage. It circled once above us and then flew on out over the sea towards Samson.

I knew at that moment what was going through Daniel's mind and knew I had to forestall him. 'There's no one in there, Daniel,' I said quickly. 'You can tell there's no one there. Let's go on and see if the boat's in Great Par. No need to go any closer is there? Well I'm not going up there, that's for sure.' And suddenly all those terrible fears of the Birdman welled up inside me once again.

'You can stay here if you like,' Daniel said ignoring my protests, 'but I'm going to find out if he's in there. What's the matter with you, Gracie? What's he ever done to hurt you? I mean we know he's not mad now, don't we? Come on, Gracie, it'll be all right.'

I found myself following him reluctantly up the hill, through head-high bracken and heather into the biggest and best-kept vegetable garden I had ever seen and past a pair of white beehives that stood like sentries on either side of the track. Several brown hens ran squawking towards us out of the heather and then followed us up the path at a discreet distance. We slowed, almost tiptoeing as we reached the front door that blew shut in our faces just as we reached it. Daniel knocked once. No one came. He knocked again.

'See?' I said, pulling him back. 'He's not there. I told you, didn't I? I told you he wouldn't be.' But Daniel paid me no attention. He lifted the latch on the door, took my hand firmly in his and we stepped together into the darkness of the cottage.

It was one long room with an unmade bed at one end by the fireplace, and an ornate black stove at the other. And above the stove on the mantlepiece stood *Woodcock,* the bright blue boat we had made for him. At the back of the fireplace was a pile of dead grey ash that the wind from the open door was whipping about the room. Daniel shut the door behind us to keep the hens out. Almost the entire room was taken up by a long trestle table that was covered from end to end in carvings, bird carvings, finished and unfinished, and around each one of them was a group of pencil sketches pinned to the table. Some of these had been torn away by the wind and a few of the carvings had been blown over onto the floor. The floor itself was a mat of wood shavings and sawdust, and the stone walls around were lined from the ceiling to the floor with shelves that bellied under the weight of hundreds of carvings. We were being watched by a silent audience of gulls and kittiwakes, petrels and gannets, merlins and puffins and plovers. Some were diving, some were preening themselves, but most stood glaring angrily at us from the shelves as if we had interrupted a secret meeting of bird conspirators.

To one side of the stove were the only shelves in the room not filled with birds. Instead on each of the four shelves there was a loaf of bread. I noticed that not much was left of the loaf on the bottom shelf. I was glad to have Daniel's hand to hold, nothing could have persuaded me to let go. He led me over to the stove and felt it. 'Cold,' said Daniel. 'They haven't been back all night. We won't find his boat in Great Par, Gracie; we won't find it anywhere.'

'They could still be on Samson,' I whispered. 'Couldn't they? I mean that's what I'd do; I'd wait there till the sea was calm and it was safe to come back. That's what you'd do, isn't it?'

Daniel shook his head. 'The oar, Gracie. Where did the oar come from if they're still on Samson?'

'But it needn't be theirs, need it?' I said. 'Could be someone else's, couldn't it?' Daniel did not answer me. A sudden gust of wind shook the cottage, rattled the windows and whistled down the chimneys disturbing the ash in the fire grate. I moved closer to Daniel who had picked up the end of the loaf on the bottom shelf to smell it.

'Wonder why he keeps four loaves?' he said. Then, as if they were all answering together, the birds lining the shelves began to shriek and scream at us. That was more than I could take. Dragging Daniel behind me I ran for the door which opened in front of us just as we reached it. Prince was suddenly around our legs, jumping up at us and shaking himself all over us; and blotting out the light from the doorway was the black, hooded silhouette of the Birdman with a kittiwake perched on his shoulder. Above him I could see the sky was white with screeching gulls. Daniel and I backed away towards the stove knocking over a chair as we went. Prince followed us sniffing at the bread in Daniel's hand.

'Hungry, were you?' came the voice from inside the sou'wester. 'Plenty of bread, always make plenty of bread. Bake one a day. Always have plenty in reserve in case I get ill. I keep the freshest till last, on the top shelf – you can have some of that if you like.' The kittiwake lifted off his shoulder and landed clumsily amongst the carvings on the table, knocking one of them over. He hopped on one leg; the other seemed curled up and stunted and he would not use it. The Birdman shut the door behind him, pulled off his sou'wester and shook it dry.

'Bit of a bluster out there I can tell you,' he said. The words he spoke were unformed and unfinished. They seemed yawned out rather than spoken and then thrown out from the top of his mouth. He heaved his black cape off his shoulders wincing as he did so, folded it and laid it carefully on the floor. All his movements were painfully slow and stiff. He whistled sharply and Prince left us at once and sat down on the cape, looking from the Birdman to us and back again as if waiting for someone to say something, but no one said a word.

We must have spent a full minute looking at each other. The old man I saw in front of me was not at all as I had expected him to be. All my life I had thought he would have the predatory look of an ancient crow under the shadow of his sou'wester. I could hardly have been more wrong. Only the tired stoop of his body and the loose, mottled skin of his forearm betrayed his age. His face was the colour of a well-worn polished brown boot. The skin was creased but still young and supple – not that you could see much of his face for it was almost entirely hidden by a head and beard of wild white hair. But it was his eyes that marked him out from any other man I had ever seen for they drew you into them somehow so that you could not look away even if you wanted to.

'So, at last we meet,' he said, breaking the long silence. 'I'm glad you came. I was afraid you never would you know. 'Course I could have gone down to the beach I suppose, but then you'd have run away soon as you saw me coming, wouldn't you? Not allowed to get too close to me are you? "Keep your distance" – is that what they told you? I don't blame them. Everyone runs away from me. I'm quite used to it by now; but I didn't want to risk that, not with you. That's why I sent Prince here down to see you and I hoped he would bring you home with him one day, but you never came. I thought of inviting you, of leaving a message in the sand asking you to come and visit; but then I thought that might frighten you away and you'd never come back.'

Still neither Daniel or I spoke. The kittiwake on the table glared evilly at us first with one eye, then the other.

The Birdman shook his head. 'Bit of a mess in here, isn't it?' he said. 'Course if I'd have known you were coming today I'd have tidied the place up a bit. Mother always said there was no one as untidy as I was; but I haven't had anyone up here in this house since she died, and that's nearly thirty years ago now. Nothing much to tidy up for if you never have visitors, is there? I mean they don't mind, do they?' And he laughed, looking around the room at the birds on the shelves. 'The wind blew the door open again by the look of it; ash everywhere. Still, not too much harm done though. One day I'll have to get round to mending the latch on that door. Been meaning to, but there always seems to be something else to be done. Never enough hours in the day.'

He stood looking at us and a smile opened his mouth. He did not have many teeth. 'What a gale that was last night, wasn't it? I can tell you I was lucky. Half-way across to Samson I was when it hit us. Came in faster than I thought it would. Only just made it. The dog came with me of course – always does, don't you boy? He always likes to go over to Samson. Likes the rabbits he does, and there's rabbits everywhere over there, great big black ones. Oh, he loves his rabbits. Course I don't often go out in the boat nowadays, only across to Samson when I have to. I can't pull against the wind like I used to – getting old you know. I spent the night over there like I usually do. Only one cottage left with a roof on it now, not like it used to be I can tell you. Made a fire, kept ourselves warm, didn't we, Prince?'

At the mention of his name, the dog looked up from

cleaning a paw, his wet tail slapping against the wall behind us. 'Then this morning, first light, with the wind around behind us and the worst of the storm blown out I thought we'd try to row back. Thinking about it now, I suppose I should have waited an hour or two but I had the goats to milk, and the hens to feed. Had to get back for them, poor old things. And if I leave Friend alone for too long he goes off all over the island looking for me. All the way up to Shipman's Head he goes – dangerous up there, even for a donkey. So I had to get back. I tell you though, I never had to pull so hard in all my life, did I, Prince? Then this old wrist had to go and give up on me.' He held up his left hand and flexed his gnarled fingers slowly. 'It just seized up, nothing I could do about it. Couldn't hold onto the oar any more, couldn't grip it. Worst of getting old – your body won't do what you tell it any more. It was just off the Point out there. We nearly ended up on the rocks after that, didn't we Prince? I had to paddle my heart out with one oar. Don't know how we managed it, but we did, and the waves brought us nicely into Popplestones. I looked up and there was old Friend himself waiting for me, as if he knew I was going to beach there all the time. So I had a ride home and here I am. And I'll tell you something else for nothing, I wasn't the only thing washed up on Popplestones. I've never seen anything like it. The whole beach is covered with timber, great thick pine planks they are, finest looking timber I've ever seen; and no sign of a wreck that I could see, just the timber.'

'Gracie found the oar,' Daniel said, but the Birdman

did not hear him. He raised his voice a little. 'She found the oar, Mr Woodcock, the one you lost. It's still down there in the dunes; we left it there. We thought you were done for, didn't we, Gracie?'

A sudden troubled look had come over the Birdman. The smile that had lit his face until now trembled and vanished, and he turned away from us while Daniel was still speaking. He lowered himself carefully onto his knees by the fire and began to break up the pile of lightings. Daniel and I exchanged glances. 'That's why we came up here, Mr Woodcock,' Daniel went on, 'to see if you and Prince were all right, because we knew you went off to Samson yesterday. We saw you rowing out there. Then when the storm came last night we thought . . .' The Birdman still had his back to us and seemed intent on lighting his fire. The paper flared and he bent down to blow on it until the flames were shooting up through the lightings into the chimney. He sat back on his haunches and watched it. I nudged Daniel, willing him to go on talking, but he shook his head. I mouthed to him silently, 'The war, tell him about the war.'

Daniel nodded and tried again. By this time the Birdman was sitting on the corner of his bed holding his hands out and rubbing them together in front of the flames. 'Mr Woodcock,' Daniel began, even louder now to be sure he was heard, 'you know we told you what Welly Belly said? You remember he thought there was going to be a war soon? Well they started it, Mr Woodcock, just like he said they would. They started it yesterday. It's all right though. Everyone seems to think we'll win it fairly quickly, but we've got to be on the look-out now for ships and submarines and things just in case we get invaded – that's what my father told me. And we're not allowed to show any lights at night. We have to draw the curtains.'

The Birdman looked up, his face filled with resignation. He put his hands on his knees and pushed himself up until he stood looking down at us again. 'You can talk all you want, Daniel, but I won't hear a word of it, not a word. These old ears of mine don't work like they should, haven't done since I was a boy. Mother always said it was the fever that did it, the fever I caught the day we left Samson. All I remember was the ringing in my ears and the roar of an endless wind blowing through my head. I could hear after the fever went, but the world was always muffled to me after that. As the years passed I heard less and less, and now these last couple of years I can't even hear my gulls. All I can hear is an empty silence. I'm as deaf as my wooden birds over there, Daniel. I can read though – Mother saw to that – but you know that already, don't you? So if you've got something to tell me, you'll have to write it down or draw it. Got plenty of paper – keep it for drawing the birds.' And he reached into the drawer of the little table by his bed and took out a pencil and a sheet of paper and put them down on the table beside us.

'You spell better,' said Daniel, handing me the pencil. 'You tell him.' So I wrote in my best writing: 'They began the war yesterday.' And Daniel turned the piece of paper round so that the Birdman could read it. When he looked up again there was anger in his eyes.

'It's wrong,' he said. 'It's all wrong. All killing is wrong, I tell you; I should know better than anyone. I should know. I should know.' And then as if he had suddenly had enough of us. 'Time you were going. I've got my goats to milk and my hens to feed, and you'd better get back home and quickly. Must have been in the sea some time already that timber, maybe most of the night. Doesn't do it any good to stay in the sea any longer than it's got to you know. So you get back home now and tell them all to get out to Popplestones as quick as they can. There's cartloads of it there, I tell you, 'nough to build ten houses. You'll have to hurry else it'll be too late. Soon as the Preventative hear about it – and they always do – they'll be crawling all over the island. Off with you now.'

We were almost out of the door before he called us back. 'Children,' he said, more gently now. 'That cormorant I gave you must be getting lonely all by himself. I think perhaps you ought to have another one to keep him company – token of your first visit.' And he picked up one of the carvings off the table, brought it up close to his eyes to examine it. It was a crying gull with its wings half-opened and a flatfish on the rock under its feet. 'I don't think I can do much more with this one. Like to take it with you?'

Daniel took it from him with great care and he looked up at the Birdman, pointed at his own lips and mouthed slowly and silently, separating each word, 'It is beautiful, thank you.'

'Thank you,' I said, following Daniel's example. And the Birdman understood and laughed aloud.

'You'll come back and see me tomorrow if you can?' he said. 'Now get along with you and get that timber hidden away before the Preventative find it.'

5 THE PREVENTATIVE

WE HID THE BIRDMAN'S GULL UNDER A PILE OF RAGS on the workbench in Daniel's boatshed – it was the only place we could think of – before running back to the house to break the news about the timber washed up on Popplestones. Within a few minutes the word had spread and every cart and wagon on the island was hitched up and hurrying towards Popplestones. It was only then when I was sitting up beside Mother and Father on the cart that I wondered whether Daniel and I should have gone out to Popplestones first to be sure the Birdman had not been exaggerating, but my first glimpse of the bay was enough to reassure me. I could see the Birdman's little boat hauled up on the dry sand, and from one end of the beach to the other the sand was littered with timber. Some of it had been smashed against the rocks and lay splintered in the water, but most of it was scattered across the beach in untidy piles and was still quite undamaged. In the farthest corner of the bay by the rocks the sea itself was smothered under a heaving, groaning blanket of boards.

Any thoughts of the war were forgotten now in this new heady excitement. No one could remember a harvest such as this, and for us on the island that is exactly what it was. Life there was never easy. We lived only on what we grew, on what we fished out of the sea, on what we made and sometimes by what we found on the beaches. Whatever was washed up by the sea on Bryher was as much ours as the fish we caught or the crops we grew. It was the way we lived, the only way we could live. Just as the seaweed and driftwood belonged to whichever of us were fortunate enough to find it and carry it above the high-water mark, so it was part of the same ancient tradition that anything, any wrecks, any cargo, any trove washed up on our shore belonged to us by right. But every child knew well that the Customs Officers over on St Mary's – the 'Preventative' as we called them – had different ideas and they would do all they could to stop us from keeping such a windfall; and there was nothing that united the islanders so much as the prospect of a visit from the Preventative. Everyone knew that morning on Popplestones that the Preventative would be coming sooner rather than later – they always did.

So all that day we loaded timber onto the carts and wagons, and they went back and forth along the track under Gweal Hill to every farm and every house on the island. Many of the men, Father amongst them, were neck high in the seething sea throwing hooks and anchors over the jammed timbers to pull them apart. Then we would grab them and haul them up out of the sea and onto the dry sand. No one even stopped to eat at mid-day. No one stopped for anything, except for a few of the smaller children who soon tired of the work and set up a see-saw with one of the planks over a rock. No one minded that for they were too little to be of much help and anyway it kept them out of the way. By late afternoon the planks were all gone and only a few of us stayed behind on the beach to tidy up, to remove all traces of the day's work. Using seaweed for brushes we swept the beach from end to end, walking in a line backwards so that we covered our own tracks as we went. We smoothed over all the tell-tale footprints, hoofprints and wheelprints that had criss-crossed the sand. We had not quite finished when the Preventatives' boat was sighted by the look-out on Watch Hill, but by the time their boat reached the quay we were ready for them.

There must have been at least half a dozen Preventatives, all of them dressed in their dark blue uniforms done up to the chin with bright brass buttons. The peaks of their caps rested on their noses so that you could not see their eyes. Most of them I noticed seemed to have long black moustaches, almost as if it was part of the uniform. They spoke to no one, but began by combing the island from Shipman's Head to Rushy Bay; and then, as we knew they would, they visited every house on the island.

We did not have long to wait before our turn came and we saw one of them opening our squeaky front gate and coming up the path. Father met the Preventative officer at the door and I was relieved to see that Father was the taller and broader of the two men. I felt very proud as I always did of Father and very safe under his protection. I could tell from the way Mother's hand was shaking that she did not feel quite so secure. I stayed with her at the sink peeling potatoes as we had planned, and I listened.

'Mr Jenkins, isn't it?' said the Preventative officer.

'That's me,' said my father. 'You looking for something?'

'This is a serious matter, Mr Jenkins, not a matter for levity. It so happens we had a few timbers – nice ones they were too – washed up on the west coast of St Mary's this afternoon, Colombian pine planks. Good sound timber, about fifteen foot long, a foot wide and three inches thick. Seems like they came in from the west during the storm last night. Well they must have done, mustn't they?' I could tell from his voice that he knew we knew, and that he knew we knew he knew. It was a kind of game but a serious one.

'If you say so,' said Father.

'I do, Mr Jenkins, I do. And we think it's likely that more of this timber was washed up on the west coast of Bryher. Stands to reason, doesn't it?'

'Ah well,' said Father, 'I wouldn't know about that. You see I hardly ever go over that side of the island – no one does – dangerous over there you know. Anyway I suppose you've had a good look over there yourselves, haven't you?'

'We have indeed, Mr Jenkins.'

'Find anything did you?'

'No, Mr Jenkins.'

Father shook his head and tutted. 'That's a pity,' he said. 'That's a terrible pity. Still perhaps all there was came up on St Mary's. Perhaps that's all there is.'

'I don't think so, Mr Jenkins, and it's my duty to remind you that any such timber would be the property of the Crown and it would be a felony to remove it or conceal it from the proper authorities. A criminal offence, Mr Jenkins, a criminal offence. And we are the proper authorities.'

'But there isn't any timber, is there? I mean you couldn't very well miss great planks of wood that size, could you?'

'No, Mr Jenkins, you couldn't.' And the Preventative officer straightened his shoulders and stretched himself to his full height before he went on. 'I have to ask you formally, Mr Jenkins, whether you have come across any such timber?'

'I wish I had, and if I had you'd have been the first person I'd tell, you know that. I'm a law-abiding man – we all are on Bryher.'

'Of course, Mr Jenkins, I've never been on an island more law-abiding than this – that's if you can believe what I've been told on every doorstep I've visited. No one I've spoken to has seen anything. But I wonder if your little girl here can help us? Children have such keen eyes, don't they, Mr Jenkins? Perhaps she's seen something you might have overlooked. Come over here little girl, don't be frightened.'

Mother took my shoulders and turned me round to face him. The Preventative was quite portly and almost purple in the face, whether with fury or exertion I was not sure. I was nervous certainly but not frightened, for Father was there behind him smiling over his head at me and I was confident I could play my part in the conspiracy. All I had to do was to keep a straight face and play ignorant. But it was then that I saw the white mess on the top of his cap and the dribble of it running down his left shoulder. One gull at least disliked Preventatives as much as we did. I did try not to laugh, but I did not succeed. A stifled squeak came out rather than a laugh, but it was recognisable as a laugh and quite enough to upset him.

'There something funny, little girl?'

'No, sir,' I said. It was not only the bird-spattered cap that made me quite unable to control myself, it was the thought of those hundreds of pine boards lying hidden under the pathways in the flower pieces and potato fields all over the island. It had been Father's brilliant idea and it must have worked, for otherwise the Preventative would not still be searching. Every sixth row in the daffodil piece was left as a path. It was here, and in between the rows of potatoes that the boards had been laid end to end and covered over. The flower pieces were untended and weed-covered at this time of year so they had even replanted the weeds to make it look right – the first and last time, Mother had said, that she would ever do that.

The Preventative officer's face had gone a deeper shade of purple. 'This is a serious matter,' he said. 'There is nothing funny about this at all.' And with some effort he crouched down in front of me so that our faces were on the same level. He forced his face into a kind of smile; but it looked to me more like a snarl than a smile. 'You can tell me where they've hidden them, can't you, little girl?'

Again my lips would not obey me and I could not hold my laughter back. His face darkened with anger. It was Mother who saved the situation.

'It's your cap,' she said sweetly. The Preventative officer took it off and it was clear he was not at all amused by what he found, but it seemed it was enough to explain away my laughter. Mother tried to make amends by taking it from him and wiping it with a wet cloth. However, the man's dignity had been ruffled and he was not finished with us yet.

'Well if you've nothing to hide, Mr Jenkins, then you won't mind will you if I search the house?' And he took his cap back from Mother and set it firmly over his eyes again.

'What? Search my house for fifteen foot wooden planks?' Father said. 'Where on earth are we going to hide things that size in a little place like this?'

'Oh you'd be surprised, Mr Jenkins,' he said. 'You'd be surprised at the places I've found things, I can tell you. I'll start like I always do, start with the roof and work downwards. Plenty of room under the thatch, I shouldn't wonder.'

'Well you won't find a thing up there,' Father said, 'except perhaps a few dead birds and mice. You'll find mice all right. But you're welcome to look anyway, I've nothing to hide. The trap-door is in my daughter's bedroom, just above her bed. It's the only way into the roof. Nothing to hide, have we, Gracie?' And Father smiled reassuringly at me as he led the man upstairs.

But my laughter had died suddenly inside me. Until they mentioned the roof it had simply never occurred to me the Preventative officer might want to search there. The roof was the only secret place in the house, the only place no one ever looked into, the only place I could hide anything I wanted and be sure it would never be discovered. That was why I had hidden the Birdman's cormorant up there. It had been the perfect place for it, hidden yet available. Every evening before I went to sleep I would climb up onto my bed, lift the trap-door and take it out to look at it and touch it; and whenever Daniel came to the house we would take it down and admire it together in the secrecy of my room.

I could hear them walking now across the bedroom floor above my head. The boards creaked and I knew exactly where they were. 'It's all right, Gracie,' Mother said putting her arm around me. 'He'll soon be gone.' Then I heard the trap door grate as it was lifted off and waited for the cormorant to be discovered. I did not have long to wait.

'Well, and what have we here, Mr Jenkins?' came the Preventative's voice. 'Didn't you say there was nothing up here?'

There was a long, long pause and then father began to speak in a voice so low that I could not hear a word. They talked together for some time up there before I heard the trap-door drop back into place and their heavy tread coming down the stairs. Father came first holding the cormorant in both hands and he was laughing as he came into the room. 'Well, I did say there were only dead birds up there, didn't I? Look what we found, Clemmie,' he said. 'Quite a surprise after all these years, isn't it? It's been lost for so long, we'd almost forgotten we had it. God knows how many years it must have been up there in the roof, and if you hadn't come here today looking for those planks we'd never have found it again. I'm very grateful to you, sir. You haven't seen this before, have you, Gracie? My father, your old grandfather, made this over fifty years ago now. Never thought I'd see it again, never thought I'd see it again. You remember it Clemmie, don't you?' Mother seemed stunned for a moment. All she could manage was a weak smile and a nod, and then I looked away from her for fear of catching her eye.

After that the Preventative made only a half-hearted search under the settle and under the table and then, feeling perhaps that his honour had been sufficiently restored, he left us. Father shut the door after him and turned round to face me. I looked from Mother to Father and back again. Of the two I think Father looked the more angry, but I always feared Mother's silent disapproval more than his roaring anger.

'Well?' he said, holding the cormorant out under my nose. 'And where did you get this from, Grace Jenkins? I want the truth now mind, none of your stories.'

'Daniel and me, we made it,' I said.

'You made this?' Father said, his voice rising to a shout. 'You don't expect me to believe that do you?'

'Honest,' I insisted. 'We did, we did. You can ask Daniel if you like. He'll tell you.'

Mother took the cormorant out of Father's hands and looked at it closely. She handled it gently. 'Gracie,' she said quietly, 'how can you say such a wicked thing? You know Daniel couldn't make this. I know he's clever with his hands but he's not that clever. This is the work of a craftsman, a real craftsman. Daniel couldn't do this.'

'And anyway,' Father went on, 'what was it doing hidden up in the roof? Answer me that if you can, Grace Jenkins.' Father's brow was furrowed and I could see his anger taking hold.

I was crying anyway by now, so the tantrum I threw came easily to me, as did the lie. 'All right then; if you don't believe me, I'll tell you. It was going to be a Christmas present and I hid it up there so you wouldn't find it and so it would be a surprise and I wish I'd never done it now and I never will again and I'll never give you anything else ever again.' I ran crying up the stairs, leaving my mother and father silent in the room behind me.

They left me where I was, sobbing noisily on my bed. Then almost at once I heard the front door open and shut and Father's footsteps going away down the path. From my bed I could see him striding along the escallonia hedge down towards Daniel's boatshed. I buried my head in my pillow again, knowing that this was the end of it all, knowing that I would have to tell them everything now about the Birdman and about Rushy Bay. Once they discovered I was lying I would have no other choice. I could just see the shed door from where I was. I lay there on the bed and waited for Father to come out. When he did, Daniel was with him and Father was carrying the seagull the Birdman had given us in both hands.

'Clemmie isn't going to believe this,' I heard Father say. 'She's not going to believe this when she sees it. Clemmie! Clemmie!' he called and Mother came out of the house and met him half-way down the path. Father held out the seagull and she took it carefully and turned it over and over in her hands. 'He made this too, Clemmie,' Father said. 'Daniel made this one too.'

'You make this yourself, Daniel?' she asked.

Daniel nodded. 'I can't do puffins though,' he said sweetly. 'I keep trying to do a puffin. I started six of them now but I can't ever get them right. Look.' And he held out his half-finished lumpy-looking puffin. He had contrived a look of bemused bewilderment as if he could not understand what all the fuss was about.

'And you made the other one too, Daniel, the cormorant?' Mother asked. I could hear she was still not convinced.

'Well not on my own; Gracie helped me of course,' said Daniel. 'You know, like she helps me with the boats.'

'I should have thought puffins would be easier to carve than cormorants or gulls,' Mother said. 'And who taught you to carve like that anyway?'

'Taught myself,' Daniel said.

'That's just how they are when they've caught a fish and they're trying to keep it for themselves,' said Father stroking the raised wing of the seagull. 'You ever seen anything like this before, Clemmie?' But Mother never answered.

'Can Gracie come out now?' Daniel asked. 'Everyone's going down to the quay to see the Preventatives off.'

'I'll call her,' said Father. 'Gracie,' he shouted up to me. 'Daniel's here.'

I came slowly down the stairs rubbing my eyes, still sniffing as convincingly as I could. Father was waiting for me by the door. He put his arm round me as he led me outside. 'Been a bit of a misunderstanding, Gracie,' he said. 'Perhaps you'd better go and put that cormorant of yours back in the roof. We'll pretend we never saw it, shall we? And we'll have it for Christmas just like you planned. I never would have believed you two could make something like that. Forgive and forget, eh?' And he hugged me tight, and kissed me with his tickling beard that always smelt of smoked fish and pipe tobacco.

All the way down to the quay I never spoke a word to Daniel. I hardly dared look at him, for I knew Mother must still be suspicious and that she would detect any flicker of collusion between us, but I could not resist just one quick glance. Daniel looked back at me po-faced but I recognised the glee in his eyes. He blinked at me once. Daniel always blinked when he meant to wink – he never could shut one eye at a time.

When we reached the quayside the Preventative boat was just weighing anchor and half the island was there to watch them leave empty-handed. We stood in the silent crowd until the boat was well out into the channel, and then a spontaneous cheer of relief and triumph went up and did not stop until we knew they could hear it no longer. I think I must have cheered louder and harder than anyone else there, but then I did have more to cheer about.

6 THE KING'S SHILLING

THE ELATION THAT FOLLOWED THE DISCOVERY OF the timber on Popplestones did not last for very long, for as the months passed the shadow of the war grew ever closer to the islands and began to darken all our lives. Talk of the Front in France soon became as common as talk of pilchards or crayfish, lobster or potatoes, and as important to all of us on the islands as the weather itself.

At home, as the news came in of more ships sunk and more retreats on the battlefields in France, Father became ever more despondent and angry. All the joy and exuberance he breathed into our lives at home vanished during that first year of the war. He rarely smiled even at me and he never set me up on his shoulder as he used to do on the way back home when we had been out fishing together. Indeed he took me out with him less and less now. He said it was too dangerous with the German submarines lurking out there in the Atlantic – and it was true they had been sighted quite close to the islands – but that was not the reason, and I knew it. He just wanted to be on his own. At home in the evenings he would scarcely ever speak to us and when he did he often spoke harshly to Mother. I had never before heard him speak unkindly to her. He would sit in silence by the fire, rolling his pipe in his teeth, staring vacantly into the flames, and the house became a place of gloom around him. Mother tried her best to lift Father's spirits and to placate his rages, but could do neither. No more could I.

It was from Mr Wellbeloved at school that I learnt about what was happening at the battlefronts in France. Frequently now the blackboard at school became the battlefield of the Western Front. I welcomed these extended lectures on the progress of the war because at least it meant we might be missing an arithmetic lesson. Like some omnipotent Greek god, he pushed and wheeled the great armies to and fro across the blackboard, forecasting with great conviction our inevitable and total victory. He told us that even if we were not winning yet we soon would be because God was on our side. Mr Wellbeloved talked with great pride and fervour of the bravery of our little army holding its own against the German hordes sweeping through France. We could help our soldiers, he said, by making blankets and socks for them; and so we did. I remember he wrote out messages of exhortation and stuffed them down the socks we had made before packing them away in boxes to be sent off to the Front. But socks, he said, were not enough. We had to be vigilant, and report at once anything, anything at all that looked suspicious. Invasion, he said, was always possible. We had to be prepared.

Whether it was Mr Wellbeloved's words that inspired the war games, I am not sure; but I do know that it was Big Tim who organised them up on Watch Hill. With rifles and bayonets whittled from driftwood, the two armies, one British and one German, would be drawn up opposite each other on either side of the hill. Big Tim would blow a blast on the battered bugle his uncle had brought back from the Boer War, and that was the signal that would send the two armies screaming towards each other over the heather. The battle that followed was always swift and the outcome always the same – after all it was Big Tim that picked the sides and he made quite sure the British always won. Either the Germans would run away or they would fall, dying noisily on the spongy grass around the rabbit warren at the bottom of the hill; and Big Tim, dressed in his uncle's pith helmet and waving the union jack, could always be seen standing triumphant on the battlefield at the end of the day.

Of course they tried to make us join in, but we had no wish to be cannon fodder in Big Tim's war games and besides we were always far too busy building our boats and sailing them – that was what we told everyone and they had no reason to doubt us. In fact, of course, we slipped away as often as we dared to the Birdman's cottage on Heathy Hill.

For Daniel and me his cottage became a second home

during the first year of the war. I was happy enough frolicking with Prince along the sand on Rushy Bay, or kneading the Birdman's dough for him in the wet weather when his fingers were too stiff and painful. The Birdman never asked for help. He was just the kind of person you wanted to help. I suppose that was why I offered to milk his goats for him. It looked simple enough, and I had milked a cow before after all. A goat was smaller than a cow, so it had to be an easier job I thought. I was wrong, very wrong. Goats know. They know everything. You can see in their eyes they know everything. They knew I was clumsy and inept and they made it as difficult as possible for me. One of them, Bertha it was, always walked away whilst I was milking her; and Betsy would turn around and chew my hair, pulling at it until I had to stop milking her because it hurt me so much. Only then would she let go. I was determined to master the Birdman's goats; but they knew that too and so I never did. All summer I tried. I tried gentle persuasion, I tried bribery, but milking always became a trial of will and strength which I invariably lost.

Sometimes Daniel would come with Prince and me down to Rushy Bay and we would sail our boats together as we had always done, but more often than not now he would stay inside the cottage with the Birdman and work on his carving all day long. I would leave them sitting side by side at the long table, chiselling away at an unpromising block of driftwood only to return some hours later and find the beginnings of a gannet or a plover or an oystercatcher hatching out of the wood. To me it was always a miraculous metamorphosis. They worked together with great concentration, even urgency, for Daniel was ever eager to practise and to learn, and the Birdman seemed equally anxious to teach him. I remember him saying once: 'I want to pass on all my father taught me whilst my fingers still obey me, and they won't for much longer.' The more Daniel improved the more he seemed to enjoy it and the more time he would spend carving with the Birdman. As they worked the Birdman would talk and talk. He was making up, he said, for all the years he had only had the birds, the animals and himself to talk to.

I myself was never comfortable talking to the Birdman in those early days for he would stare uncannily at me whilst I was speaking, trying to read the words as they came out of my mouth. So I would resort almost immediately to pencil and paper, partly to avoid those piercing eyes of his. Daniel never did that. Right from the very start he mouthed the words, contorting his lips into extravagant shapes. He made letters out of his fingers and spelled out the words. He drew shapes in the air; indeed sometimes he did all three at once and talked aloud at the same time. If at first the Birdman could not understand – and he often did not – then Daniel would persist resolutely until he did. Sometimes this might entail acting out a complex charade, and both of them would end up helpless with laughter at his antics and the misunderstandings they created.

It took some time and it was gradual, but Daniel invented that year a whole new private language of signs, pictures and signals that the Birdman could recognise and understand immediately, so much so that I sometimes found the Birdman could understand what Daniel was saying now before I could. I remember that at one time I began to feel a little excluded, even hurt by this; but the Birdman seemed to sense my unease and took great delight in teaching me the new sign language he was learning. We became so used to using the new language that in time Daniel and I could talk to each other without uttering a word, and we would use it at home now instead of whispering whenever anyone else might be about and we wanted to talk about the Birdman or Rushy Bay. In time though the Birdman learnt how to read our lips well enough to understand most of what we said. We had to speak slowly of course and make sure he was looking at us before we began. We still used our secret language, but he needed it less and less as the months passed.

We found out early on that there were some things you just did not talk about to the Birdman. Any mention of the war for instance, any talk of the latest outrage or offensive Mr Wellbeloved might have told us about, and he would simply turn his back and walk away. It seemed to plunge him into a deep despair and so we learned never to talk of it. Neither, we discovered, would he ever talk about himself. If we asked him about his mother or his father he would just turn his head away and pretend he could not hear us.

Then one day Daniel asked him about Samson. 'It's not really true there's ghosts on Samson, is it, Mr Woodcock?' The Birdman stared at him. 'You know,' Daniel said and he put a blanket over his head and drifted around the room arms outstretched, his muffled moanings and groaning interspersed with giggles. 'Like this, Mr Woodcock. Ghosts. Gracie believes in them, but they're not true are they, not really?' It was the only time I'd ever seen the Birdman angry. Terrified at this sudden fury, I backed away until I felt the wall behind me and could go no further. He advanced on Daniel, pulled off the blanket, took him roughly by the shoulders and shook him.

'Ghosts!' he cried. 'Ghosts! Do you know what a ghost is? Well I'll tell you. A ghost is a soul so darkened with shame and sin that it can never rest. It is a spirit condemned to wander the earth until the end of time. Yes, there are ghosts on Samson. You cannot see them, you cannot hear them, but I know they are there. They are all there, all the guilty men of Samson, my father with them.' His voice was full of anguish as he went on. 'His spirit is still there on Samson. They all are and they always will be unless the curse of Samson can be lifted, unless I can save them. Until then that place is cursed, so keep away from it. Stay away both of you.' After that I never dared mention Samson again, and nor did Daniel.

For fear of discovery we could not spend as much time as we would have liked with the Birdman. We knew it strengthened our alibi if we were seen from time to time to be sailing our boats on the pool under Gweal Hill; and now the swans had finally left we could do that again. In Daniel's boatshed that first spring of the war I busied myself repairing and repainting our fleet of boats whilst Daniel worked tirelessly on yet another puffin carving.

This was the seventh; he had rejected all the others. It would be finished, he said, only when it was perfect, quite, quite perfect. Each of them seemed to me to be more puffin-like than the one before and I would have been proud to have made any of them, but he was never satisfied. He made endless puffin sketches and pinned them to the table in the shed just as the Birdman had taught him he should.

It was while we were working side by side in the boatshed one drizzling May morning that we heard a distant dull boom. We took very little notice of it at the time. We thought that perhaps one of the Navy ships might be firing a practice salvo out to sea – we had heard them often enough before – and we had seen several grey warships cruising in and out of the islands of late, their turrets bristling with guns. Not until Father brought back the news the next day was I to find out what it was.

He had been off to St Mary's that morning to sell our catch of lobsters and crayfish as he always did on Wednesdays providing the sea was calm enough. Mother and I were down on the rocks fishing for wrasse when we saw him bringing the boat in over the sandbars towards the quay. We watched him throw out the anchor and leap down into the shallows. We could see as he came along the beach towards us that a change had come over him. He walked briskly over the sand, jumping from stone to stone and hurdling the ropes and anchor chains as he came. I could feel Mother's arm come around me, and I knew she was bracing herself for something, but I had no idea what it might be.

'Clemmie,' he called as soon as he was within ear-shot. 'Clemmie, I've done it and I feel ten years younger for it. Should have done it long ago.' He was smiling now as he used to and I wondered why it was that Mother was looking away from him as if she did not want to hear what he was about to tell her. 'You remember that explosion we heard yesterday morning? Well, they sank another freighter, Clemmie,' Father went on, 'not five miles from here it was. Submarine again. Just waiting out there they were, and they picked her off and sent her to the bottom. All good men, all gone. They told me all about it over on St Mary's as soon as I arrived this morning. I saw for myself a couple of lads laid out there on the beach. Washed up on the tide this morning they were. They were young lads, both of them, barely out of school, half my age, Clemmie. Well that was it, that was enough. I decided there and then I wasn't going to stand by any more and just watch. It isn't right, Clemmie, you know it isn't. They need sailors and I'm a good one, better than most. We Scillonians are the best navigators in the world; we have to be, don't we? So anyway, I went and signed the papers, Clemmie. There's a dozen or more joining up from all over the islands, but I'll be the first from Bryher. It's all done. I joined the Navy. I've taken the King's Shilling.'*

Mother's arm tightened around my shoulder and I looked up at her. She was smiling at him. 'I'm not going to argue with you,' she said. 'You wouldn't listen to me

* To 'take the King's Shilling' is to join up. In fact, volunteers received a day's pay when they joined up, which was about a shilling.

anyway, would you? I knew you'd be going sooner or later, I knew it had to come.'

'You won't go short, Clemmie,' said Father. 'I've worked it all out. I'll be sending money home all the time. Pay's not bad you know, one and a penny a day. You and Gracie won't even need to work the flowers and potatoes if you don't want to. There'll be enough for the both of you, don't you worry.'

'I'm not worried about that. I'm not worried about the money,' said Mother. 'Gracie and me can manage till you get back, can't we, Gracie? We'll see to the flowers and potatoes; might even catch a few lobsters, you never know. It's not just men that can catch lobsters you know. No, it's you I'm worried about.'

'Me?' said Father. 'Stuff and nonsense.' And he picked me up and set me high on his shoulders. 'Getting heavier by the day, Gracie,' he said as I put my arms around his neck. 'You used to hang on to my beard when you were smaller, remember? It's a wonder I've got any left.' And we walked back up to the house, happy together for the first time in months. 'Don't you worry about anything, Clemmie,' he said. 'I'll be back before you know it. Won't take long this war, not now I'm in it.'

'No dear,' said Mother. 'Not now you're in it.' And she put her arm around him and laid her head on his shoulder.

'When will you be going to the war, Father?' I asked from high above them.

'Soon,' he said.

And it was soon, all too soon. Only a week later

Mother and I were standing on the quayside at St Mary's and Father was hugging me to him. He looked so fine and grand in his blue uniform. Maybe it was my pride in him that stopped me crying like everyone else seemed to be. I tugged his beard when I kissed him goodbye and he laughed and then whispered, 'Take care of your mother for me, Gracie.' I remember thinking that was all the wrong way round, for Mother had always been the one to take care of me. And then he laid a hand on Mother's arm, brushed her cheek gently and said, 'Bye, Clemmie. Chin up.' And he was gone, up the gangplank and into the ship.

We waited until the ship was so far out that we could no longer distinguish him from the others waving beside him on the deck. 'At least he's his old self again,' said Mother, taking my hand and leading me away. 'At least he's happy now.'

'They won't sink his ship, will they?' I asked Mother on the way back across the water to Bryher.

'Course not, Gracie, don't even speak of it. He'll be back, you'll see.'

I told the Birdman the next day that my father had gone to be a sailor in the war and he smiled sadly and put his hand on my head. 'Daniel and me will look after you,' he said. 'We'll look after you and your mother, won't we, Daniel? I'll be your father till he gets back home again; how would that be?'

'That'll be fine,' I said. 'Just till he gets back though.'

7 SAMSON

NOTHING WAS EVER TO BE THE SAME AGAIN AFTER Father left. I basked briefly in the reflected glory of a father away fighting in the war, but the void he left behind him grew wider and deeper as time passed. The glory soon faded as it always does, and when other fathers went off to the war I found I was no longer even very special.

At first we did manage well enough on our own, Mother and I. She insisted everything had to go on just as before. 'One day soon,' she told me, 'any day now, your father will come in through that gate and up the path and I want him to find everything just as he left it. Meanwhile we have to live, don't we?'

So to that end she toiled all day and every day working up the fields and planting, bringing in the seaweed to dress the flower pieces and often going out lobster fishing alone in the boat whilst I was at school. I begged to be allowed to stay away from school to help, but perhaps she suspected my reasons were not entirely unselfish for she would never hear of it. She sent me off to school every day that summer. So I had to endure Mr Well-beloved whether I liked it or not, and I left Mother behind to do both her work in the house and Father's work outside all on her own.

There was less time than ever now to go visiting the Birdman and Prince and no time at all to sail our boats on the pond. The boats gathered dust and cobwebs in the back of Daniel's boatshed, and when Daniel was not helping us out in the fields – and he often did – he went by himself to the cottage on Heathy Hill. I tried to console myself with the thought that at least I would not have to milk those horrible goats, but there was little enough comfort in that. I missed Prince and I missed the Birdman. Each time I saw Daniel go off alone I longed to go with him, but I knew I could not. My place was at home now alongside Mother, so I stayed behind.

As summer passed into autumn Mother became ill. The long hours of work in the fields and out in the boat were taking their toll of her strength and her cough settled on her chest and forced her to stay indoors in the warm. I could see her back was troubling her as well. She found it difficult even to let herself down into her chair at the end of the day. She tried to disguise it from me of course, but she could not. Only Father's letters, infrequent and brief as they always were, seemed to brighten her life and keep her from despair. She would read them aloud to me over and over again and then put them up on the mantleshelf over the stove beside the Birdman's cormorant I had given them for Christmas. I often noticed that she would look up at them during the long dark evenings as if she were trying to draw strength from them.

It was on those rare happy days when Mother had just received a letter and when all the work was done that I felt I could leave her and go up to the Birdman's cottage with Daniel like we used to. Whenever I went there now the Birdman would greet me like a long lost friend, sitting me down on the edge of his bed by the fire and feeding me a great feast, a cup of warm goat's milk and all the bread and honey I could eat – and I could eat plenty. Every mouthful seemed to give him as much pleasure as it gave me, if that were possible. He would sit opposite me in his chair nodding and smiling until I had finished every last crumb. I remember that kittiwake on his shoulder watching me enviously with his beady sideways eye. I did not care for that bird and I could tell from the way he looked at me that the feeling was mutual. I would suck the honey deliberately noisily off my fingers so that the kittiwake would know what he was missing.

The Birdman was as good as his word. He was indeed a father to me, looking after Mother and me like some anonymous guardian angel. Often, first thing in the morning when Mother went down to open the door, she would find a loaf of bread on the doorstep, or perhaps some eggs or potatoes or milk, and occasionally a huge jar of honey. 'Manna from Heaven,' she would say, dipping her little finger into the jar and licking it. 'Manna from

Heaven. People are so kind. But we can't live on charity, Gracie. Your father wouldn't like that, wouldn't be fitting.' I longed to tell Mother who our benefactor was, but I dared not for fear she would forbid me from ever going to see him again.

I often tried to thank the Birdman for his kindness, but either he pretended not to understand or he seemed to sense what I was about to say and would turn away and ignore me. In the end I had to write it down on paper for him and make him read it.

'Thanks for the honey,' I wrote in big letters, and drew a swarm of bees over the top.

He smiled at me. 'Thank the bees,' he said.

'Thanks for the eggs.'

'Thank the hens,' he replied.

'Thanks for the milk.'

'Thank Betsy and Bertha,' he replied. And I made a face at that and held my nose.

'Thanks for the bread,' I wrote.

'Thank God for that,' he said.

Daniel would bring us back the occasional fish he had caught off the rocks at Droppy Nose Point, so thanks to the two of them we never went hungry, Mother and I. But winter was coming on and Mother was worried; and it was not just about whether we would have enough food to last. 'It's the money, Gracie,' she confessed to me one night, lying beside me in bed – we had taken to sleeping in the same bed since Father left. 'Your father sends me all he can, but one pound and ten pence a month just isn't enough. I had to buy in seed potatoes and bulbs this year, and then there were those repairs to the boat. I've got to keep the boat going, Gracie, for your father when he gets back. And the lobster catch was poor for everyone this year. The few I did manage to catch no one wanted to buy. There's no market for them now. It's the war I suppose. Oh, Gracie, how I hate this war for what it's doing to us all. And then there's still the rent to pay. I could manage if only I was strong enough to go out and do a bit of fishing. A few good catches a month and a bit of luck and I could sell enough fish to bring in enough money to keep us going.'

'I could do it, Mother,' I said sitting up beside her. 'I could go fishing, course I could. Daniel would go with me, Mother. We'll take Father's boat out and we'll bring back all the fish you need. I've done it with Father often enough, haven't I? I know where to go. And Daniel can handle a boat as well as anyone; you know he can, Mother.'

'No, I can't let you,' Mother said. 'And Daniel's too young anyway. You're both too young to go out fishing alone. We'll manage, I expect. We'll be all right. When I get stronger, Gracie, we'll go out together.'

'Please, Mother.'

'No, Gracie,' she said. 'It's out of the question. It's October already. Summer time it would be different perhaps, but if you get out there this time of the year, and the wind gets up you'd not come back. We'd lose you and the boat and then what would I tell your father when he comes back home? No, you're not to do it, Gracie. You hear me? It's too dangerous.' But I knew there was no other way to find the money she needed, and I knew Daniel would need little persuasion.

The next evening, a still overcast evening with the sea the same soft grey as the sky, Daniel and I took out one of his father's boats. It was smaller than ours, a fourteen foot lugger that Daniel thought we could handle more easily. We said nothing and told no one for we knew they would forbid it. We waited until the beach was deserted and slid the boat out gently into the water. We set sail as soon as we were round the point and out of sight of the houses, and then made out past Samson round Droppy Nose Point towards Scilly Rock. 'Best place for pilchards,' Daniel said. 'Father always says so. We'll be back before dark and no one will ever know we've gone. You can always tell your mother I caught them off the rocks, can't you?'

So we baited our hooks, let down the lines and within half an hour we had caught more fish than we had ever dreamed of. Two dozen pilchard or more and one large bass. We were fishing midway between Gweal and Scilly Rock. Perhaps it was the one big bass that tempted us to stay just a little longer to see if we could catch another even bigger. Whatever it was, we were so intent on our fishing that we never even noticed the weather coming in behind us. We were fishing with our backs to Scilly Rock and the open sea. The boat lolled beneath us, lapped by a listless sea. I had just hooked my biggest pilchard when I noticed a wisp of mist above our heads. I looked around over my shoulder. Scilly Rock had vanished as had the sky and the sea as well. A grey wall of fog was rolling in towards us over the sea. There was nothing we could do, for it was already too late to do anything. It was over us and all around us before Daniel could even haul up his line. Gweal and Bryher beyond it were not there any more and we were left alone and lost on a silent sea. What little breeze there was had gone and we found ourselves quite becalmed. I remember we spoke in a whisper, as if the fog were a living creature that might be listening to us. I was not too worried though, not at first, for the sea slapped so softly against the sides of the boat and seemed to hold no threat for us. Besides, I had Daniel with me. Both of us had been out in fog before, and both of us thought we knew the waters around Bryher quite well enough to get home.

'As long as we keep Scilly Rock astern of us we can pull home easily enough,' Daniel said softly.

'But how are we going to do that if we can't see it?' I whispered, taking the oar he was handing me. 'I can't see it any more.'

'We can hear it though, can't we?' he said. 'Listen.' And certainly I could hear the surge of the sea seething around Scilly Rock as it always did even on the calmest of days. 'Hear it?' he said. 'Just keep that sound astern of us and we'll be able to feel our way home. Gweal must be dead ahead from here. There's no swell to speak of, so we won't go on the rocks. All we have to do is to hug the coast all the way round and that'll bring us nicely into Popplestones.'

And so we began to row, only a few strokes at a time, stopping to listen for the sea around Scilly Rock. It was not long though before I began to think that Gweal was not at all where it should have been. We had already been rowing quite long enough and hard enough to have reached it by now. Then I thought that perhaps the current must have dragged us off course, that we must be somewhere between Samson and Bryher, that I could still hear Scilly Rock somewhere astern of us and distant, but Daniel was no longer even sure of that. We pulled until our arms could pull no longer, but still no land loomed up out of the fog as we expected. Within half an hour we had to admit to each other that we were quite lost. We sat over our oars and drifted, straining our ears for the wash of the sea against the rocks, anything to give us some idea of where we were. The fog though seemed to obscure and shroud the sounds of the sea just as it was hiding the islands that we knew lay all around us. Even the piping of invisible oystercatchers was dulled and deadened as the dark came down through the fog and settled around us.

Strange as it may seem, the darkness came as a kind of comfort to us, for at least it was the kind of blindness we were accustomed to. Even Daniel who was never fond of the dark seemed relieved at the onset of night. We searched now for some crack in the blackness about us, a glimmer of a light from the shore that would guide us safely home. We sat beside each other huddled together and silent, the damp jibsail wrapped around us to keep out the cold, peering constantly into the impenetrable night and listening, always listening for the hiss of surf on the shingle or the distant muted charge of the waves against the cliffs.

Often during that long, long night our hopes were raised by the whisper of waves on some far shore, and we would row frantically towards it for a few minutes and then sit silent and listen again, only to discover it had been nothing but wishful thinking, a trick of the mind. Either it was that or we had simply been rowing the wrong way – we could never be sure which. In this dense darkness all sense of direction, time and space seemed to be distorted. Each time our hopes were raised only to be dashed, and each time the disappointment was all the more cruel and all the more lasting.

The cold had numbed my feet up to my knees and my hands could no longer feel the oar I was pulling. I wanted so much just to go to sleep, to give up and go to sleep. But Daniel would not let me.

'Got to keep moving, Gracie,' he said. 'We don't know where we are, do we? We only know that we're cold and that we're going to get colder if we just sit here, so we're going to row. We're going to row till we warm up and then we'll rest and then we'll row again. We might be rowing out to sea but at least we'll keep warm. We can't just sit here.' And so we did, Daniel calling out the rhythm to keep us together.

I discovered that night that you can sing almost everything there is to sing to the rhythm of the oars, that is if you change the rhythm of the song. We were half-way through 'Ten Green Bottles' for the second time when I saw the light and stopped rowing. It was a flickering prick of light, the kind you see when you close your eyes tight shut and look into the back of your eyelids. I did not believe it at first for I did not want to be disappointed again, but when Daniel saw it too, I knew my eyes were not deceiving me. Then at last we heard the welcome sound of the sea running back over the sand.

The boat beached even before we saw the shore, the bottom grating and growling to an abrupt halt in the surf. We jumped out and pulled her out as high as we could on the next wave and then dropped the anchor into the sand. Both of us believed that we were on Popplestones until we discovered there were no pebbles above the line of sand as there should have been. We found instead we were climbing in amongst dunes. Then hand in hand we were stumbling up through dead bracken and heather towards the light that shone in the sky ahead of us like some glowing orange moon as we approached it. Daniel stopped often to call out, 'Is there anyone there? Anyone there?' But his voice was deadened by the fog-black night, any echo stifled. I heard only one reply, the single bark of a dog somewhere far away in the darkness.

'Prince?' I called out. 'Is that you, Prince?'

'You're imagining things,' Daniel said. 'It was nothing, I never heard anything. Come on, let's get up to that light.'

It was a long, painful climb. The sharp heather tore at my legs as I followed Daniel up the hillside. The dark shape of a cottage grew out of the gloom and we ran towards it; but there was no door, no windows and no roof. Just an empty shell was left, the walls, a fireplace at each end and the window-ledges. Through one of the windows I could see the light flaring high above us. As we came out of the cottage and turned towards the light, our footsteps were suddenly loud in the night, crunching over what we found to be a mound of limpet shells. I thought at first that what I was hearing must be the freak echo of the crackling of the shells under our feet, but then I smelt the smoke and I saw the first lick of orange flame flickering up into the blackness. Our light had become a great spitting beacon of fire and we ran towards it, caring no longer now for our sore legs, and calling, calling to whoever was up there. But no one was. The fire was a towering teepee of flame that was gradually falling in on itself as we watched. The heat from it sent shivers of welcome warmth through our cold aching bodies and we jumped up and down in the light of it and laughed aloud with joy and relief.

It was some time before we had warmed up enough to collect our thoughts and begin to worry again. We were sitting cross-legged up-wind of the fire, revelling in its heat when Daniel said, 'Gracie, I don't think we're on Bryher. I mean, d'you know any cottage on Bryher like that one we saw down there, that one without the roof? You seen one like that on Bryher?'

'P'raps we're on Tresco then,' I said.

'Gracie,' Daniel went on, breaking a stick and throwing it onto the fire, 'there's only one island where there's houses like that. Samson, Gracie. I think we've landed on Samson.'

Until then I hadn't given a thought as to where we might have landed. I had not cared. I was happy just to be safe, alive and warm again. 'It can't be,' I said, moving nearer to him; and as I looked around me, the darkness seemed to close in on us. 'You sure?' I whispered.

'I'm sure,' he said.

8 CASTAWAYS

THE FIRE WAS OUR ONLY COMFORT THROUGHOUT the long and dreadful hours of the night. Each new settling of the burning embers sent an explosion of sparks high into the sky until all that was left was a perfect circle of glowing embers. Only fear kept us awake, fear of the unknown out there in the dark around us, and fear that one of us might fall asleep and leave the other to face the night alone. Every rustle behind us in the heather, the sudden squawking of a disturbed gull, even the soft groaning of a seal in the bay somewhere below us kept us both taut with terror. We talked all night long, as much as anything to keep out the noises of the night around us. I sought endless reassurances from Daniel and he did indeed seem to have an answer for everything. It was just that sometimes I found it difficult to believe him.

'You think the Birdman's here then?' I asked. 'How do you know it was him that lit the fire?'

'Well, he's the only one who ever comes to Samson, isn't he?' Daniel replied. 'And someone built this fire, didn't they? It has to be him, stands to reason. And remember you were the one that said you heard Prince barking just after we landed. They're here somewhere, got to be. Soon as it's light, we'll find the house he stays in – the only house on the island with its roof on still – that's what he told us, remember? All we've got to do is find it and he'll be there. He can't leave the island in this fog any more than we can, can he? Don't worry, Gracie.'

'But I still don't see why he lit this fire,' I went on. 'Not unless he's signalling to someone out at sea. P'raps that's it, Daniel. P'raps that's what he's up to. He could be, couldn't he, Daniel? I mean that's what those smugglers and wreckers used to do in the old days, isn't it? That's what I heard.'

'A smuggler?' Daniel laughed. 'The Birdman a smuggler? Don't be silly.'

'Could be,' I said. 'Why not?'

'Gracie,' Daniel said. 'If you were a smuggler and you were signalling to a ship out there, would you do it in thick fog?'

'All right then,' I went on. 'If you know so much then, you tell me why he's gone and built a fire in the middle of nowhere?'

'Who knows?' Daniel shrugged his shoulders. 'P'raps he's frightened of the dark. I know that's what I'd do if I found myself alone here in the middle of the night.

Anyway, it's his island, isn't it? I mean he lived here, didn't he? He can do what he likes. He can build fires anywhere he likes. You still don't trust him, do you, Gracie? Not after all he's done for us, you still don't trust him.'

'And what if he isn't here at all?' I said. 'What if we don't find him in the morning? I mean you'd think Prince would have heard us by now and come and found us, wouldn't you?'

'He's here, Gracie, honest he is. You'll see.'

'But what if those stories are true?' I said, lowering my voice to a whisper. 'What if all Father told me is really true and Samson does have a curse on it, like Charlie Webber told him. What's going to happen to us then? You've only got to set foot on the island and you'll be cursed for ever. That's what he said. That's what hapened to Charlie Webber.'

'Tommyrot,' said Daniel. 'It's all tommyrot. Everyone knows it's just stories.'

'Then why doesn't anyone else ever land on Samson if it's all stories?'

'They're just scared, that's all,' Daniel said. 'Just scared.'

'Well so am I,' I said. 'It's this place, Daniel, it doesn't feel right. And it's not just the dark either. I'm not the one who's scared of the dark, am I? There's ghosts here, Daniel. I can feel them all around us. The Birdman told us, didn't he? And one of them's his own father. That's what he said, didn't he?'

'Just imagining things I expect,' said Daniel. 'I mean if

you were alone on this island for long you'd begin to imagine things wouldn't you? And after all he is old, isn't he? Anyway he never said he'd *seen* a ghost, did he?'

'No, but . . .'

'Well then,' Daniel said. 'Listen, Gracie, you ever seen a ghost? Have you?'

'No.'

'So if you've never seen one, how do you know they exist? You don't, do you?'

'P'raps not, but . . .'

'Well then, if you've never seen them and you don't believe they exist, you know he was just imagining things. Must have been, mustn't he? And all those stories your father told you about curses and houses burning down and the scarlet fever, they're just stories, Gracie. I mean everyone thinks the Birdman's mad, don't they?'

'Yes.'

'Well, is he?'

'No.'

'And Big Tim said you'd catch his madness if you touched him. Well you've touched him, haven't you, and have you gone mad?'

'No.'

'Well then. Stands to reason, it's all just stories like I said. I mean, you can't believe in anything you can't see, can you? Well can you?'

'Anyway p'raps we've got nothing to worry about,' I said. 'P'raps we're not on Samson at all.' But I knew full well we were. I could feel it. I could feel the ghosts watching us. They were out there in the darkness. I knew they were. I huddled closer to the fire hugging my knees, and prayed and prayed.

It seemed that on Samson it was the terns that decided when morning should come. It was they who announced the dawn even while it was still dark, filling the air with their raucous racket. If other birds joined in, we did not hear them. Terns ruled on this island, and the night knew it of old and left us swiftly. We had hoped that the fog might be gone by daybreak so that we could get back home, but there was no wind to blow it away and we knew well enough that autumn fog could hang about for days at a time over the islands, particularly over Samson. But it was not as thick as it had been the evening before. At least now we could see quite clearly for ten paces or so ahead of us. The terns flew shrieking in and out of the fog above our heads, fleeting pale grey shapes that seemed startled and angry to find us there; and once they found us out they never left us alone diving out of the fog at us until they drove us away from our dwindling fire. Neither of us wanted to leave it and face the dank cold of the island and I more than Daniel dreaded our meeting with the Birdman. I knew how angry he would be to find us on Samson. I was for getting back to the boat at once and making for Bryher and home, whatever the weather.

'It'll be easy enough now we know where we are, won't it?' I said. 'After all, it's only a narrow channel between Samson and Bryher.'

'Gracie,' Daniel said. 'If we get out in that fog again it'll be like yesterday all over again. You think you know where you are but you don't. We can't go, not yet. Father would kill me if I wrecked his boat. I'd prefer to face the Birdman, even if he is cross with us. But he won't be. I know him. We'll tell him we couldn't help it. And we couldn't, could we? After all, we didn't mean to land on Samson, did we? It's not as if we were snooping or anything, is it? It just happened; he'll understand. Come on, let's find him. Let's find that cottage, he's bound to be there.' Daniel was adamant. There was nothing I could do when Daniel was adamant and I knew it.

We began by whistling for Prince, hoping his bark might lead us to them and save us the trouble of searching the entire island, but only the terns replied. We tried calling, hands cupped to our mouths, but there was no answering bark. So we started to search. We followed the hill upwards from the fire and searched the higher ground first, for the fog seemed to be less thick up there. Every cottage we came to we found deserted and roofless. Fog curled out of gaping windows and doors so that each one looked like some ghostly apparition. They were elongated human faces that breathed out smoke from staring eyes and gruesome grinning mouths. I refused to go inside any of them. I would wait outside on the huge mounds of limpet shells that we found outside each cottage, while Daniel went in on his own to see if the Birdman was there, but he never was. All he ever found were a few rusting kettles and pots, a pair of shoes white with mould and some broken clay pipes. Of the Birdman and Prince there was no trace.

Every ruined cottage we came across gave me fresh

hope, hope that we might not be on Samson after all. If it was Samson, then there had to be a cottage with its roof still on – the Birdman had said as much – and we had not found one. So when Daniel emerged from yet another crumbling cottage saying he was sure we must have searched every cottage on the island by now, I spoke out. 'Then p'raps you're wrong,' I said. 'P'raps this isn't Samson at all. Could be it's St Martin's or St Agnes for all you know.' But Daniel answered me by pointing over my shoulder into the fog behind us.

I turned round and there not more than twenty paces away over the bracken I could just make out the outline of a cottage, a cottage with a roof and two chimneys. 'That's it,' Daniel said. 'That's his. That's the Birdman's cottage. Don't know how we missed it before.' And he ran past me and into the bracken, fighting his way through until he reached the cottage and threw open the door. 'Prince!' he called out. 'Prince!' I stayed where I was, and not just because I was fearful of the Birdman's anger. I was seized with a sudden terrible foreboding. My last vestige of hope had been wrenched from me. We were on Samson. There could be no possible doubt about that, not now. I was cold and tired but the shudder that went through me had nothing to do with that. It was as if some cold hand had touched me and left its curse on me. I could hear Daniel walking about inside the cottage. No Prince ran out to greet me, nor were there any gulls lined up along the roof as there most certainly would have been had the Birdman been there.

'He's not here,' Daniel said from the doorway. 'There's

no one here. He's been here, though. The ashes in the fireplace are still warm and I can smell Prince. And there's something else here, Gracie. Come and look, quick,' he said, and he went inside again. I hesitated. 'Come on, Gracie,' he called out. 'Come on.'

Inside, the cottage looked almost the same as the Birdman's cottage on Heathy Hill. There was one long table, a fire at one end and a stove at the other; but here there were two beds, in opposite corners of the room. One bed was unmade and the mattress rolled up, and on the other the blankets were thrown back against the wall. There were shelves all around the room, but they were empty. 'Look,' Daniel said, pointing to the mantelshelf above the fireplace.

It rested above the mantelshelf on wooden supports. At first glance I thought it was a lance or a spear of some kind. Thick as the handle of an axe at one end, it spiralled towards a sharp point at the other. It reached across the entire width of the cottage, overlapping the mantelshelf at each end. As I came closer it seemed to me to have been carved from a paler wood than the carvings back in the Birdman's cottage on Bryher. The surface gleamed in the cold light as if it had been varnished. 'What is it?' I asked.

Daniel reached up and touched it gently, almost tentatively. Then he ran his fingers along the horn from end to end. He did not turn round. 'Come and feel it, Gracie,' he said.

I knew as I touched it that it was not made of wood – it was too smooth and too cold. We looked at each other. 'That's real bone isn't it?' I said. And suddenly I saw what it was. 'It's off a unicorn. It's off a real unicorn.'

'Couldn't be,' Daniel scoffed. 'Couldn't be off a unicorn. There's no such thing.'

'Then what else could it come from if it isn't a unicorn?' I asked.

'Well I don't know, do I?' said Daniel, and he reached up again and tried to lift it off the supports. He could hardly move it. 'But I can tell you one thing for sure, Gracie, it's not off a unicorn. Too big for a start. Only place you'll see a unicorn is in pictures and storybooks, and I've never seen one big enough to have a horn this size. And don't tell me it's off a giant unicorn 'cos I don't believe in giants any more than I believe in unicorns. The Birdman will know. He'll tell us what it came from.'

'Where is he?' I said. 'He's not here, is he? He's not on the island.'

'Doesn't look like it,' Daniel said, still preoccupied with the horn.

'Then who lit the fire?' I asked. But he did not answer.

He turned to face me. 'I'm thirsty,' he said suddenly. 'You thirsty? People lived on this island once,' Daniel said, 'so there's got to be water hasn't there? Must be a well somewhere; only got to find it. Come on, Gracie.' And he walked out of the cottage, not even looking behind him to see if I was following. I took a last look behind me at the horn above the fireplace and ran out after him.

We searched all over the hillside around the cottage but could find no well; so we were forced to look further afield. The longer we looked, the more thirsty we became. There was no talk any more of curses or ghosts or unicorns. We argued only over where it might be best to look next, for we were now craving for water and could think of nothing else. We must have trudged the length and breadth of that island several times that morning. From the top of the hills where the fog was beginning to clear we could now look down and recognise Samson below us. Fog still covered the neck of the island, so it looked as if the twin hills of Samson were two tiny islands surrounded by a sea of fog.

The search proved fruitless. We were sitting dejected and silent on the top of a hill looking over to where we knew Bryher must be, hidden under the fog. I was thoroughly exhausted and miserable by now and could summon up neither the strength nor the enthusiasm to continue the search. I just wanted to go home.

'Let's go back to the boat, please Daniel,' I begged. 'Let's not stay here any more. I hate this place. Let's go back to the boat, please.'

'Gracie,' he said suddenly, and he was hauling me to my feet. 'That's it, that's it. Why didn't I think of the boat before? All right, so we can't drink; but we can eat, can't we? Look, Gracie, we can't leave till the fog lifts, you know we can't; but we can't just sit here and wait, can we? So why don't we have breakfast?'

'Breakfast?' I said.

'Pilchards, or bass,' Daniel said, a triumphant grin on his face. 'Take your pick. We've got a fire, haven't we? Still hot enough to cook on; bet it is. And we've got fish, back on the boat, haven't we?'

The promise of food was enough to banish at once

both my thirst and my exhaustion, and we ran together down through the high heather towards the fog-covered beach below where we had left the boat the night before. The hill was so steep and I was running so fast that my legs finally could not keep up with me any longer and I tumbled headlong into the heather, rolling over and over until I came to rest at last in a clearing of soft grass covered in a sprinkling of rabbit droppings. When I sat up I saw Daniel on his hands and knees beside me. He was not at all concerned with my welfare; but was parting the bracken in front of him.

'It's a well, Gracie!' he called out. 'It's a well! We've found the well.'

It had been dug at the foot of the hillside and was lined all around with stones. Together we peered over the edge, but it was too dark to see anything. I reached down with my hand to touch the water, but there was nothing there. Daniel picked up a large stone and dropped it down, but there was no answering splash. We heard it bounce once, twice. It was stone on stone. The well was quite dry. Daniel sat back on his heels. 'P'raps that's why the people left here,' I said. 'You can't live on an island without water.' And then Daniel was on his feet again.

'Never mind,' he said, 'we've still got the fish.'

We chose to eat the pilchards because they were small and would cook quickly we thought, but the smell of them was so good and we were so ravenous that we only half-cooked them, eating the outside of each one and throwing the rest to the gulls and terns to keep them happy. I never much cared for pilchards and I haven't ever since, but that day on Samson we ate them until we were full and no fish ever tasted so good. I think we ate as much wood ash as we did fish but neither of us cared.

I was wiping my hands on the grass when I first noticed the rabbit. It was sitting looking at us out of the bracken only a few feet away, and it was perfectly black. It seemed quite tame so I thought I would try to get closer. I was crawling slowly towards it and was within inches of touching it when Daniel shouted out, 'Gracie! Gracie!' The rabbit bolted into the bracken and disappeared. Daniel was on his feet and laughing. I was surprised and angry at him for frightening the rabbit away. 'It's going, Gracie, it's going!' he shouted.

'Course it's going,' I stormed at him. 'What d'you expect a rabbit to do if you shout at it like that?'

'Not the rabbit,' he said. 'Not the rabbit, Gracie, the fog! The fog! Look, Gracie, it's going!' And sure enough below us was the infinitely wonderful sight of the sea shimmering blue through the mist below us.

'Let's go home, Gracie,' said Daniel. And he did not have to ask me twice.

9 31ST OCTOBER 1915

WE COULD NOT LEAVE SAMSON BEHIND US QUICKLY enough, although now with the sunlight on it, it had lost its haunted look. It was only now that I was on the way back home that it occurred to me how worried Mother must have been all this time. How I longed to see her again. I thought no more of ghosts or curses but only of the joys of being home with her again, of how I would drink and drink and then climb into bed and pull the blankets up over my ears and go to sleep for as long as I wanted.

We both knew though the kind of welcome that was awaiting us. We knew the anger and the inquisition that we would have to face, so our relief that we were at last off Samson was tempered with a certain reluctance to arrive. I remember there was precious little wind that day, only the gentlest of breezes; so we did not bother even to set the sail. The warmth of the sun was lifting the last remnants of the fog off the sea as we rowed slowly down the channel past Puffin Island towards Bryher and home.

'Father's going to strap me, he always does,' said Daniel. ' 'S'pose I can't expect him not to, not after I took his boat; but it'll only make it worse if I tell him we were on Samson. He'd burst his boiler if he thought we'd been anywhere near the place, you know what he's like about rules.'

'What are we going to tell them then?' I asked.

'The truth,' said Daniel, 'only we just leave out the bit about Samson. Went fishing and got lost in the fog; that's all there is to it. Well, we did, didn't we? Didn't know where we were so we just sat it out until the fog lifted and here we are. Keep it as true as you like, Gracie, but for goodness sake don't ever let on we were on Samson.'

'Then we don't have to tell the Birdman either, do we?' I asked. 'I don't want to tell him. He'll be angry, I know he will be; and I don't like the look of him when he's angry. And he warned us not to go there, didn't he?'

Daniel thought for a moment. 'He's about the only person in the world I would never lie to. He's the only one I trust, Gracie, 'cept you of course. I'm going to tell him, Gracie, I'm going to tell him just the way it happened. He won't mind, honest. I know he won't.'

'Well you can tell him by yourself,' I said. 'I'm not going to see him, not until I know he isn't angry with us. And ask him about that thing we found in the cottage, that unicorn's horn or whatever it is.'

'All right,' said Daniel. 'I'll go. I'll ask him. Let's pull a bit slower, Gracie; I'm in no hurry to get home.'

They spotted us as we came over the sandbars past Puffin Island. Everyone came running down onto the beach. You could see the news spreading through the island. People were running from cottage to cottage, and then they were hurrying down towards us, so that by the time I threw out our anchor almost everyone on the island must have been there to meet us. I could see Mother in amongst them, looking pale and tired under her dark shawl. I waved to her but she did not wave back. Daniel's family were there too, Big Tim in amongst them, and it was Big Tim who came wading out into the shallows to help us haul the boat up onto the sand.

'You're for it now,' he said, and the smile on his face was more one of menace than of welcome. 'You're really for it.'

There were tears of relief at first. Mother held me to her briefly then she took me by the arm and led me away through the crowd. She did not say a word to me. I saw Aunty Mildred covering him with kisses in spite of Daniel's efforts to escape her clutches. But any tears of joy soon gave way to rage and Daniel was subjected to a barrage of furious questioning. He was immediately surrounded by his brothers and sisters, and as Mother led me up off the beach I heard behind me his father's thunderous voice. 'You wait till I get you home. You just wait. How dare you? How dare you take out one of my boats without asking me first. I'll teach you a lesson you'll never forget.' And when his mother intervened on Daniel's behalf he roared again. 'It's as much your fault as his, letting him run wild; and now look what he's done.

Every boat on the island's been out looking for him and he comes back here bold as brass after all the trouble he's caused. I'll tan him black and blue, you see if I won't.'

Mother waited until we were far enough away from the crowd before she said a word. I had shamed her in front of everyone, she said. How was she ever to hold her head up again on the island after this, with everyone thinking *she* had sent me out fishing for her at my age! But gradually her grip on my arm relaxed and we walked on side by side in silence for some time. 'I thought I had lost you, Gracie,' she said. 'I didn't think I was ever going to see you again. I spent all last night wondering how I was going to tell your father when he got home.' She stopped, put her hand on my shoulder and then lifted my face to look into hers. 'I know why you went out in that boat, Gracie Jenkins. I can do without the money,' she said, 'but I can't do without you. If needs be I can sell the boat. We'd have enough then to pay the rent for a year or two, and we'd be able to buy in all the food we need for the winter. Your father can always build another one when he gets back. You won't ever go off like that again, will you, Gracie? Promise me you won't. Never again.'

'I promise,' I said and she kissed me on my forehead.

'You're cold,' she said. 'You're ice cold.'

'I'm more thirsty than cold, Mother,' I said. So I had my water at last, three mugs of it brimful and wonderful. She put me to bed after that with a hot stone bottle at my feet and she sat down on the bed beside me. I waited for her questions to come; but she said nothing more about it, only that for the first time since Father left she was glad he was not at home. 'He'd have hit the roof,' she said. 'But then I suppose you'd never have gone out fishing in the first place if he had been here, would you? There'd have been no need for it, would there? And if he knew why you'd gone out, Gracie, he'd have been proud of you, that's for sure, like I am.'

'He'll be back soon,' I said. 'Won't be long, Mother. The war can't last for ever, can it?'

'Can't it?' she sighed as she got up to go, gathering her shawl around her. 'Gracie,' she said, 'best not to go and play with Daniel for a bit. You're not the most popular girl on Bryher just at the moment, you know. There's plenty of people, Daniel's mother amongst them, think you've been getting Daniel into mischief. Personally I think it's six to one half a dozen of the other, don't you?'

I rarely dream, and if I do I can scarcely ever remember them; but I dreamed a dream that night after my return from Samson that was so vivid I have never forgotten it. I saw through a sunlit fog, fleeting glimpses of Father riding over the sea on a bright white unicorn. He was in his sailor's uniform and he rode so fast that his hat fell off. He was laughing when he jumped down to retrieve it. Then the unicorn galloped off into the fog and left him alone, standing on the sea. He looked everywhere for his hat but he could not find it. It did not seem to worry him though because he was laughing, laughing all the time. As he sank into the sea he was still laughing and waving at me. All that night I kept waking up and falling asleep again only to dream the same dream again and again.

I wanted to tell Daniel about my dream – he was the only one I could tell, but there was no opportunity to do so. He had been forbidden to play with me and so we only saw each other now when we went to school, and then there always seemed to be other children around us. Even in playtime at school we were not left alone. Overnight, it seemed we had become famous. We were the heroes of the hour and constantly surrounded now by admirers who wanted to find out everything that had happened to us when we'd gone missing in the fog. However much we told them, they wanted to know more and so Daniel invented more. Each time he told the story he filled it out with colourful and often inconsistent embellishments, but no one seemed to notice. They hung on his every word.

I noticed though that Big Tim and his friends never came to listen to Daniel. They stood in a huddle in the furthest corner of the playground, whispering to each other and glowering over their shoulders at us. I did try to warn Daniel that I thought they were up to something, but he ignored me. Indeed as the days passed I felt Daniel was hardly even listening to me any more. I did not know why, but Daniel seemed quite unlike himself now since our return from Samson. It was not that he avoided me. On the contrary, he stayed so close to me all day that I began to feel he was trying to protect me from something; but he had become distant towards me, almost cold. He hardly ever spoke to me and when he did it was in monosyllables, and he kept looking around him all the time as if he were expecting something to happen. Even on the way back from school, coming down our lane when we were quite alone at last, he seemed to prefer to walk beside me in stony silence. I could have told him then about my dream; but there were more important, more urgent things I had to know.

'You been to see the Birdman yet?' I asked, and not for the first time. He shook his head and looked away. 'When you going then?' I went on. 'You said you were going to ask him about that horn thing in the cottage, you said you would.'

'Soon,' he said, and he walked on down the lane towards home, his hands deep in his pockets.

'Your father strap you?' I asked him. He nodded, but said nothing more. 'Does it hurt still?'

'Bit,' he said. 'See you tomorrow.' And he ran off up the path towards his house.

'Watch out for Big Tim,' I called after him. 'He's hatching something; I know he is, Daniel.' He waved his hand over his head and went inside.

At the time I put it down to the beating his father had given him. It had to be that; I could think of no other reason why he should suddenly have become so quiet and so sad.

Terrible things happen on quite ordinary days and there is never any warning. It must have been a week, I suppose, after we came back from Samson. I met Daniel as usual at the gate that morning and we walked together up the lane to catch the boat to school. We always went the long way because Big Tim and his friends went the short way and we always liked to keep well away from them. It was a gusty autumn morning with the leaves chasing each other in crazy circles down the lane. I remember Daniel was behaving even more strangely than usual. He kept glancing behind us, and then just before we joined the others on the boat he said quietly, not looking at me at all, 'Gracie, if anything happens at school today, just keep out of it. Don't say anything no matter what happens, understand?' There was no time to ask any whys or wherefores, no time even to reply.

It was a rough, buffeting crossing to Tresco, but I liked it that way. It took longer and there was always just a chance that if it got worse in mid-channel we would have to turn round and go back home again, but it did not. Big Tim sat in the bow of the boat with his friends as he always did; but then I saw that he was staring at us and grinning. They all were. There was menace in their eyes. I looked at Daniel and found him glaring back at his brother. There was a look of utter contempt on his face.

In assembly, Mr Wellbeloved thundered his daily tirade against the brutal German enemy, and we all sang 'God Save the King' as lustily as usual. Then in his arithmetic lesson we all had to recite our seven times table aloud. Of all of them this was the one I loathed and dreaded the most. I managed to stutter my way through it but it was not good enough and he told me to stay in after lunch and write it out twenty times. At break-time I followed Daniel out into the playground. We went and sat down together, as we often did, by the coalshed. I tried to ask Daniel again about the Birdman. 'You told the Birdman yet about Samson? You asked him what the fire was for?' But he never had time to answer me. They were all around us, about ten of them in all; and Big Tim stood above us against the sky, his thumbs hitched over his belt. His head was in the sun, but I could see the cruel grin was still on his face. I had never really looked at Big Tim until then, not closely. I suppose that was because I had grown up with him and was too used to him to notice him. Above his high collar his face had the look of a sweating red pudding; but as I got to my feet it was not his face I was looking at, but the massive fist clutching his belt. He grinned at me and pushed me back against the wall. Daniel stepped between us.

'Leave her be,' he said. 'She's nothing to do with it.'

'You're in it together,' Big Tim said. 'You're always together, isn't that right? If you're guilty, she's guilty.' And there was an ugly chorus of agreement from his friends behind him.

'Guilty of what?' Daniel said. 'All right, so you saw me coming out of the Birdman's cottage last night. What's the harm in that?'

'But that's not the half of it, is it, Danny boy?' Big Tim went on, an unpleasant sneer in his voice. 'A Hun-lover, that's what you are. I've got a Hun-lover for a little brother. No use denying it, Danny boy.' And he put a hand on Daniel's chest and pushed him back against the wall beside me. 'We saw you. We seen you often, haven't we? And not just last night, Danny boy. Keep a good look-out, Welly Belly said, for King and country, and so we did; and what did we find but my little brother running down along Rushy Bay and up into the Birdman's house on Heathy Hill. A stroke of luck really you see, 'cos we been watching that house the last few days, keeping an eye on him. Do you know why, Danny boy? Well of course you do. That friend of yours, that Birdman, he's the only one on Bryher who doesn't close his curtains at night like he should. Now why d'you think that is, eh?' And he pushed Daniel harder against the wall. 'Well I'll tell you why, it's because he's a spy. He's a Hun-loving spy and he's signalling to German submarines out at sea, that's why; and that makes you the friend of a spy, doesn't it, Danny boy?'

'Don't be silly,' said Daniel, 'he wouldn't do that. He doesn't even like the war. Says no one ever wins a war anyway, so there's no point in fighting it. He doesn't want anyone to win it.'

'Doesn't he indeed? So he's a Hun-lover just like I said he was, a Hun-lover and a spy.' Big Tim's friends closed in around us. He went on, 'Father's going to find this all very interesting when I tell him. He'll tan you again, Danny boy; that's after I've finished with you.'

'You can tell Father what you like,' said Daniel, 'but you can't prove anything. Just leave the Birdman alone. He hasn't done anyone any harm. Leave him alone, d'you hear me? The only reason you can see lights from his cottage is 'cos he hasn't got any curtains, that's all.' Big Tim looked a little taken aback at this.

'No curtains?' he said. 'That's no excuse. Got blankets, hasn't he? Everyone's got blankets. He could put up blankets. He's a spy right enough and you're in it with him, both of you are.'

'Can't you understand?' Daniel said. 'He hates the war,

says it turns men into savages. He doesn't even care who wins or loses.'

'Doesn't care, eh?' said Big Tim taking Daniel by the ear and twisting it viciously. 'So he doesn't care who wins the war? That's what we thought, isn't it, lads? So here's what we're going to do, Danny boy. When I get home I'm going to tell Father all about you and the Birdman, and he'll tell the Navy and they'll come and search his place and question him till he tells everything. And if he doesn't come up with the right answers then you know what happens to spies, don't you? They shoot them, them and their friends.' And he twisted Daniel's ear even harder, forcing him down onto his knees. The silent tears on Daniel's face at last spurred me to action and I threw myself at Big Tim, lashing out with arms and legs; but it was to little effect. He did have to let go of Daniel but then he just held me out at arm's length and laughed at me as I flailed pathetically, my arms far too short even to reach him. Then someone called out that Mr Wellbeloved was on the prowl; so he grabbed my arm, twisted my wrist up behind me and pushed me to the ground beside Daniel.

'That's where you both belong, in the dirt like all Hun-lovers. You won't see him again; he'll confess and tell them everything. I shouldn't like to be in your shoes when you get home this afternoon.' And he was gone.

Daniel helped me to my feet. 'I told you to stay out of it,' he said, his hand cupping his ear. 'I told you, didn't I?'

'But they won't shoot him, will they?' I said.

'Course not, Gracie. They'll find out he didn't do anything, not on purpose anyway; they're not stupid like

Big Tim. But we're both in trouble now. Big Tim will tell everyone all about us and the Birdman, and they'll try to stop us from ever seeing him again – you can be sure of that.'

'Daniel,' I said, brushing myself down, 'why did you tell me you hadn't been to see the Birdman?' He didn't answer me. 'You told me you hadn't been and you had.' He looked at me and then looked away again quickly.

'I didn't want to have to tell you, Gracie.' He spoke quietly, almost as if he were talking to himself. 'He was going to tell you himself, Gracie,' he said. 'It's about the curse, the curse of Samson. It's like you said. It's like your father told you. It's all true, but there's more . . .' And just then Mr Wellbeloved appeared round the corner.

'Anything the matter?' he asked.

'No, Sir,' said Daniel.

'Then run along in. Break's over. Bell's going.'

After lunch I had to stay in to write out my seven times table twenty times; and Mr Wellbeloved kept me at it all afternoon, sending me back and back to do it again until I got it right. But I never did get it right. I kept making small mistakes, for my mind was not on my work that day. I was not thinking of Big Tim and having my arm twisted again, I was thinking only about the curse of Samson. Would it be me or Daniel to suffer the curse first? I wondered if the house would be burnt down when I got home. I wondered if Mother would be sick with the fever, or whether we would drown on the way back to Bryher. I would have to tell Mother, to warn her. I would have to tell her before someone else did, all about the Birdman and Samson; and I knew how hurt she would be that I had deceived her all this time. How I dreaded going home that afternoon.

The boat from Tresco dropped us at the quay as usual and we took a different way home up through the town for fear of meeting Big Tim and his friends. As we passed the houses we noticed that people were gathered whispering in their doorways and they would disappear indoors as we approached. We saw them peering out at us through their windows. Even the Vicar looked away and did not speak to us as he hurried by in his billowing black cassock, and that was most unusual for him.

When we reached my front gate Daniel's mother was waiting there and she took him roughly by the arm and whisked him away into the house. 'What's the matter?' he asked. 'What've I done now?' but she said nothing, and I noticed she seemed not to want to look at me.

Mother was sitting in her usual chair, but it was not usual for her to be sitting down at this time of the day. 'Come here, Gracie dear,' she said, her voice an unnatural whisper. When she lifted her head and looked at me I could see she had been crying. 'We've lost your father,' she said.

'Lost him?' I said.

'He's missing, Gracie,' she said and she held up a letter and handed it to me. It was a brick red envelope that I held in my hand and the address on the outside was in pencil, as was the writing on the letter I took out. It read: 'The Lords Commissioners of the Admiralty regret to inform you that J591671 Able Seaman Peter Jenkins of

HMS Louis was reported missing in action on 31st October 1915.'

'That means he's not coming back, doesn't it?' I said.

'Oh why him?' Mother said. 'Why us?'

I knew well enough the answer to that question.

10 DAWN ATTACK

I GRIEVED THAT NIGHT AS ANY CHILD WOULD WHO had just lost a father; but when I cried it was as much from guilt as from sorrow. From the moment I read the letter I had little doubt in my mind that I had been the cause of my own father's death. It was I who had set foot on the forbidden island and brought the curse of Samson down on our heads. I lay awake beside Mother all night long trying to convince myself that there was at least a possibility it had not been *all* my fault, that after all thousands of soldiers and sailors were dying in the war. But no matter how I reasoned I could not get it out of my mind that it was I and I alone that had been responsible.

Mother lay awake beside me like a statue that night consumed by her own silent, private agony. She held my hand and squeezed it whenever I began to cry but neither of us talked. I was tempted to confess everything, but I could not bring myself to do it. Anyway, I thought, there was no point in it; not now. It would not bring Father back and that was all she wanted. It was all I wanted.

The day after the letter came was a wretched day of endless visitors. Friends and relatives from all over the islands came to pay their respects. They all brought little gifts, a posy of flowers or a pot of jam; and they all smiled sweetly, said how sad they were and left as quietly as possible, some on tiptoe as if they were in church. They were all of them kind, but it seemed to me as I stood behind Mother's chair witnessing this procession that Father's death had altered every one of them, for none of them really talked to us as they used to do. They made short, hushed speeches, their eyes lowered, and then they became impatient to leave. It was as if we had contracted some dreadful contagious disease; they were sympathetic but they were keeping their distance just to be sure they would not catch it.

Only Daniel's voluminous Aunty Mildred, the aunt who was for ever kissing him, stayed to drink the cup of tea Mother offered everyone, and she talked just as she always talked. She was the only one I remember who actually mentioned Father. 'Of course,' she went on, after first saying how sorry she was, 'of course he was a fine man your Peter, good fisherman, brave man; but I always said he should never have left you and little Gracie like he did to go off to the war. I told him so at the time. I said, "Peter," I said, "you're too old to be going fighting wars at your age, there's plenty of younger ones should go first who haven't got wives and children." ' She sighed, sipping her tea daintily. 'But they never listen, do they, dear? They always think they know better, don't they? You can't tell them, can you?' And when she got up to go several cups of tea later it was already dark outside the window. She hugged me to her so long and so hard that she almost smothered me. 'Poor little mite,' she said, kissing me on the head. 'Poor little mite. Anything I can do to help, you know where I am.' And she was gone.

When I shut the door behind her and turned round I saw that Mother was smiling, the grief lifted from her face for the first time that day. 'Thank God for Aunty Mildred,' she said and she closed her eyes and put her head back against the chair. 'It's a funny thing, Gracie, but I never liked that woman, not until now. Neither did your father, come to that.'

Then came a knock at the door. 'Someone else,' Mother said. 'People are kind, Gracie, they're so kind, but I don't know if I can face anyone else. I'm tired, I'm so tired.'

'Could be Daniel,' I said. 'He hasn't been yet.' But even as I was opening the door I had the feeling it wasn't Daniel. The Birdman stood there in the darkness. He smiled at me, but there was not a flicker of recognition in his face; and then Prince was jumping up at me and squeaking with excitement.

The Birdman and mother looked at each other across the room. Mother had sat up in her chair and had her hand to her mouth. The Birdman held out a pot of honey for her. 'Heard about your husband,' he said. 'I heard what happened. I've come to tell you I am sorry. Believe me, Mrs Jenkins, I am so sorry.'

'It's Mr Woodcock, isn't it?' said Mother rising from her chair and taking the honey from him. 'And I think I have more to thank you for than just this one pot of honey, haven't I? It was you wasn't it? It was you all along. You were the one who's been so kind to Gracie and me all this time.' But the Birdman was already walking out of the door, Prince following at his heels. 'Mr Woodock,' Mother called out after him, 'I've a cup of tea for you; it's still warm.' But the Birdman never even looked round. He disappeared down the path and into the darkness.

'Well,' Mother said, 'so now we know who it was. But why, Gracie? I don't understand it. I've never even spoken to him before this evening. Worse than that, I've avoided him all my life and Father always kept well out of his way too.' She was looking directly at me now, the honey still in her hand. 'He speaks so strangely. It may only have been the way he talks, but I felt that he meant what he said more than anyone else today. It was almost as if he felt responsible somehow, as if he was apologising.'

To my great relief Mother said no more about it until we were in bed later that night. 'I've been thinking,' she said, 'about that dog, the Birdman's dog. You ever seen that dog before, Gracie? Have you? He certainly looked as if he knew you, jumping all over you like that, just like you were old friends. Gracie? Gracie?' But I was as fast asleep as I could pretend to be, my breathing so deep and regular that pretence must have given way to fatigue and I was soon well and truly asleep.

I was woken suddenly. I thought at first it might be a

gull tapping on the window, but when I looked there was nothing there. The night sky was already grey with morning. I could see the branches of the tamarisk tree outside my window shaking in the wind; but there was no gale blowing and it was only in a gale that the twigs scraped against the window pane. I sat up in bed slowly so as not to wake Mother, who lay on her side facing away from me. Then I heard it again and this time I knew it for what it was, for I heard the pebble fall back and bounce on the path outside. I eased myself carefully out of the bed and crept over to the window. Daniel stood on the path looking up at me and he was beckoning me to come down. I dressed quickly at the bottom of the stairs, wrapped myself against the cold of the morning and stole out of the house.

Daniel said nothing. He put a finger to his lips to prevent me even from whispering. We stole down the path and out of the gate and then we began to run. We ran all the way up to the top of Samson Hill before we stopped to rest. I looked across to the Birdman's cottage, but everything was dark on Heathy Hill. I flung myself down exhausted in the heather and Daniel crouched down beside me. 'Won't help saying anything I don't s'pose,' he said, 'but I am sorry, Gracie, honest I am.'

'It was the curse of Samson, wasn't it?' I said, and he nodded. 'My father's dead and all because we went on that island, isn't he? It's all true, isn't it?'

'The Birdman told me everything,' Daniel said. 'But it's not his fault, Gracie, and it's not your fault. He's done all he could.'

'What do you mean?'

'Tell you later Gracie. There's no time now. We've got to warn him; we've got to warn him quick.'

'Warn him?' I asked.

'It's Big Tim and his crowd,' Daniel went on. 'I heard them planning it. Dawn attack they called it. You remember what he said at school, don't you? Well Big Tim went and told Father, just like he said he was going to. He told him I'd been over to see the Birdman and all that tommyrot about the Birdman being a spy and signalling to German submarines. 'Course Father believed him, Father always believes everything he says. He strapped me again and then shut me in my room – that was Big Tim's idea so's I wouldn't be able to warn the Birdman that they were coming to search his cottage. And they did come, police from St Mary's, yesterday afternoon. I heard them talking to Father outside the window when they came back from the Birdman's cottage. Course they didn't find anything and they were angry. They told Father not to waste their time in future. Said they had better things to do than go visiting madmen. A lot of silly nonsense, they said. How could anyone think that a mad old fool like that could be a spy? Didn't even understand the questions they asked him. All he'd do was smile and nod his head – couldn't even speak properly, they said. So anyway, when they left, Father turned on Big Tim and gave him a piece of his mind for making him look a fool. They let me out at teatime and I went over to see the Birdman straight away to tell him about your father. He was so upset, Gracie. Said he had to go and see you and your mother. I tried to stop him; but he had to go, he said. He had to see your mother and tell her face to face how sorry he was. Blames himself, see. I warned him you'd be in trouble if he looked as if he recognised you in front of your mother. I told him he mustn't recognise you.'

'Prince did,' I said, 'leapt up on me he did, just like he always does. Mother knows something's up, I think, but she's not sure what. I think she's too tired to care. You could have warned me,' I went on. 'You could have warned me he was coming, couldn't you?'

'I was going to, Gracie,' Daniel said. 'I was on my way back from Heathy Hill to tell you he was coming, and then I heard them.'

'Who?'

'Big Tim and everyone, like I told you. Must've been about a dozen of them there, outside the boatshed; and I could hear Big Tim planning this dawn attack, just like he was a general or something. He said they should never have sent out the police to question the Birdman. They should have sent the navy, he said. They'd have got the truth out of him. He said he knew the truth anyway. The Birdman was a spy, had to be; and of course they all agreed. If no one else would do it then he'd do it himself. He was going to teach the Birdman a lesson. The last thing he said was that they'd meet at dawn and ransack his cottage. They want to drive him off the island for ever, Gracie.'

'Didn't anyone try to stop him?' I asked.

'No one argues with Big Tim, you know that. They're all frightened of him,' Daniel said. 'So that's why we've got to get there first whilst there's still time. We got to warn him, Gracie.' And he pulled me to my feet again and we began to run down towards Rushy Bay and up over the dunes towards the Birdman's cottage. Already there was a glimmer of daylight creeping over the sea.

When we got there the cottage was quite empty. The two goats came to nuzzle us as we searched outside and it was then that Daniel noticed that the cart was not in its usual place. 'He's off collecting wood somewhere I expect,' he said. 'Popplestones or Hell Bay. We've got to find him.'

We were passing the pool under Gweal Hill when I happened to look over my shoulder and saw them, shadowy figures against the skyline, flitting through the undergrowth high on Samson Hill. 'It's them. They're coming,' I said. 'What can we do?'

'Nothing,' said Daniel taking my arm and pulling me on. 'It's too late and there's too many of them.' We ran on down towards Popplestones.

The donkey and cart were by the rocks at the far end of the beach, moving from time to time as the donkey browsed along the line of seaweed, and for a moment that was all we could make out, until we heard Prince barking. We could see the Birdman now, standing in the shallows. A flock of gulls lifted off the water and circled shrieking overhead. Then we saw a long dark shape lying at the water's edge and the Birdman kneeling in the water beside it. As we ran across the sand we could see he was trying to roll it over and that it was clearly too big for him to move. It could have been mistaken for a great log but for the fact that it moved – it moved of its own accord. It had a huge fan-shaped tail that lifted and fell, slapping the water as we came towards it. The Birdman heaved again and the creature writhed once more and lifted its head. Until that moment the horn had been camouflaged from us because it was almost the same colour as the sand. The creature, whatever it was, possessed a long, pointed horn that protruded from just below the dome of its blunt black head. It was only when we came closer that we saw how vast the creature was. From tail to head it was the length of a small boat, perhaps fifteen feet, and the horn itself half as long again. It looked more like a whale than anything else. The fine tapering horn seemed an unnatural and incongruous addition to the clumsy bulk of its body.

'The horn, Daniel,' I said. 'That's just like the horn we found in that cottage on Samson, isn't it?'

'It's just like he told me,' Daniel said quietly. 'It's just like the Birdman told me.'

'What d'you mean?' I asked, but Daniel was running on ahead of me.

The Birdman got slowly to his feet as he saw us coming. Prince had stopped barking and growling, and was bounding up the beach towards us.

'Thank God you've come,' the Birdman called out. 'I can't do it on my own, not strong enough. Been here all night trying to roll her back into the sea, but she's too heavy for me.'

'What is it?' I asked, reaching out to touch it and then not daring to do so. It was speckled black all over, but darker along the ridge of the back than anywhere else.

Daniel pulled at the Birdman's sou'wester so that he should turn and look at him while he was speaking. 'It's like the ones they killed on Samson isn't it?' Daniel asked. 'It's the same, isn't it, Mr Woodcock?'

'Just the same,' he said. 'It was me that found the first one that day too.' And he looked out to sea. 'The others will be out there at sea just like they were before and they'll come in just like they did before. They think they can help, you see, but they can't. We've got to get her back in the water before they come else they'll beach themselves just the same. We've got to do it before anyone comes, I tell you. If they find her here that'll be the end of Bryher. It'll happen all over again.'

'What will?' I shouted. 'What's going on? What are you talking about? I don't understand what's happening. Please tell me, please.' I was crying now, out of grief and bewilderment, out of anger and frustration.

The Birdman looked down at me and spoke more softly and clearly than I had ever heard him speak. 'After what happened to your poor father,' said the Birdman, 'you have more right to know about the curse of Samson than anyone else, and you shall know. But I haven't much time to tell you, so listen well, Gracie. It was all a long, long time ago but I remember it as if it were yesterday. Samson was always a poor place when I was a boy, little enough food to go round and life was hard. But we survived well enough until the day the whales came. I found the first of them lying on the beach early one morning, crying out for help. Mother and I tried to roll it back into the sea, but we couldn't move it.'

The whale shifted again on the sand and the Birdman looked round. 'Just like that one, just the same,' he said. 'And by daybreak the whole island was there, but they wouldn't help us, not even Father. And do you know why not?' I shook my head. 'Well, I'll tell you, Gracie. You see, there were more whales out in the bay and the more the stranded whale cried out, the closer the others came to the beach. The people only had to wait and they knew it. By noon all the whales were stranded on the sand, calling out to each other, crying pitifully. Mother begged them not to do it, I begged them not to do it, but it was no good. They had all made up their minds. They said there was enough ivory in the horns to make us all rich for life. So they butchered them on the beach in the sunshine, and the blood stained the sand and ran out into the sea. The sea was redder that evening than any sunset I've ever seen. The very next morning, Gracie, we woke up to find a ship out in the bay, stuck fast on a sandbank.'

'The ghost ship,' I said. 'The ghost ship Father told me about.'

'Ghost ship?' the Birdman said. 'Maybe it was. It was deserted that's for sure, not a soul on board. They couldn't believe their luck – ivory one day and a fine ship for salvage the next. They floated her off the sandbank on the morning tide and sailed for Penzance. Every man on the island went, Father too, and they took the horns with them to sell on the mainland – all except one. We found it later, Mother and me, half buried in the sand.'

'That's the one we found over on Samson,' Daniel said.

The Birdman went on, hardly pausing for breath. 'They none of them came back. I never saw Father again. The ship went down with all hands. Every man on Samson was gone. Mother said the island was cursed because they had massacred the whales, but no one believed her. They said she was mad. And they didn't believe her in the years that followed when ship after ship was wrecked on the rocks off Samson. Over fifty people have died in those wrecks, Gracie. Even the few that crawled ashore never survived. Everyone said it was just bad luck, but Mother and I knew it was the curse. When the hunger came and the disease we knew what it was, and still no one believed us. All we had to eat were limpets and a few wild rabbits.'

'Did you eat the dogs?' I asked. 'Father said you had to eat the dogs.'

The Birdman nodded. 'When you're starving you eat anything,' he said. 'One by one the other families left. For two years Mother and I lived alone on the island. Mother wouldn't leave; she didn't want to leave Father's ghost on the island. Said she owed it to him to stay. We would never have left at all if the well hadn't gone dry. Never failed before, that well. Wet summer it was, too. No, it was the curse that dried that well, Gracie. It was the curse that drove us off the island.'

The Birdman looked up towards the black hills of Samson in the distance. 'All my life I've tried to lift the curse. All my life I've tried to keep everyone away from Samson. That's why I row out there whenever there's a storm threatening, whenever I see the fog rolling in. It's to light a beacon on the clifftop to warn the ships to keep away.'

So it *was* you,' I said. 'It *was* you over on Samson that night Daniel and I got lost in the fog.'

'Yes, it was me,' he said sadly. 'And I wish to heaven I'd never done it. It was my fire drew you to Samson, Gracie and brought the curse down on you. And now your poor father's dead.'

At that moment we heard the first blood-curdling yell up on Heathy Hill behind us. We turned round. 'Look!' Daniel said, pointing up toward the hillside where we could just make out Big Tim's soldiers moving like shadows through the dark of the heather for their dawn attack on the Birdman's cottage. We saw the goats bolting up the hillside bleating in terror, and then came the sound of squawking hens and crashing glass.

'We're too late, Gracie,' Daniel said. 'We came to warn you, Mr Woodcock. It's Big Tim and his friends. Like I told you, he thinks you're signalling to German submarines. Thinks you're a spy or something.'

'Spy?' the Birdman did not seem to know what the word meant. He seemed more hurt and puzzled than angry. 'It doesn't matter, anyway,' he said, turning away. 'All that matters now is the whale. She must not be allowed to die. She must not. The tide is already on the ebb so if we don't get her back in the water soon it'll be too far to drag her and then it'll be too late.'

'They're inside the cottage now, Mr Woodcock,' Daniel said. 'I can't see any of them outside any more.'

'Let's hope they stay inside,' the Birdman said. 'It's

getting lighter all the time. If they see us here I'm afraid that'll be the end of it, just like it was on Samson when the whales came before.'

However hard we pushed and shoved, the whale always rolled back to where it came from. Daniel and I tried to ignore the sounds of destruction coming from the cottage as we threw ourselves time and again against the side of the whale. Desperately we dug the sand away from one side and tried to roll it over, but it would only go so far before the fin on the far side would push it back towards us again. All we had managed to do it seemed was to make matters worse, for the whale now lay half buried in a deep trough of wet sand, and all the time the tide was taking the sea away from us.

We sat back to regain our strength and to take stock of what could be done. We knew it was useless to try again, but we steeled ourselves for one last attempt. Kneeling in the sand, our shoulders against the side of the whale, we heaved together, once, twice; and then felt the great weight of the creature falling back on us. As it came back it fell heavily into its ditch in the sand almost trapping my arm underneath it. I was sitting breathless in the sand when I heard Big Tim's voice behind us.

'What've you got there?' They were coming towards us across the beach.

'Look at the size of it!' one of them said; and they stopped several yards away from us. Big Tim was the next to speak.

'Well, what is it?' he asked.

'It's a whale,' said Daniel, 'and we've got to get it back

into the sea before it dies. We've got to. Because if it dies the Birdman says we'll all be cursed on Bryher just like they were on Samson. You got to help us, Tim. If you all help we can roll it back, easy.'

'The Birdman says,' Big Tim mimicked, and his friends laughed in unison around him. 'The Birdman says. He's a Hun-lover, Gracie I told you, Gracie, he signals to German submarines, maybe to the very one that killed your father. Well, we've broken every window in his cottage and we've pulled down his henhouse, and there's a few of those wooden birds that won't fly again; and if he stays we'll be back again, and then it won't be just his windows we'll break – it'll be him. D'you hear that, you mad old fool? You clear out; you're not wanted on this island.'

The Birdman got slowly to his feet and limped towards Big Tim. Prince followed growling at his heels. As he came towards them Big Tim and his friends backed away. 'You must be Big Tim,' he said. 'I think I recognise you. Daniel told me all about you. I tell you, if we do not get this creature back into the sea before she dies, then this island will die like Samson did. Do you hear me? Do you understand what I'm telling you? If you love your island, help us while there is still time.'

'Help you?' said Big Tim still backing away. 'Why should we help you after what you've done? Anyway that whale or whatever it is doesn't belong to you; it belongs to all of us. If you want it for yourself, you'll have to drag it up above high-water mark, and you're too old and feeble to do that, aren't you? And these two aren't much use, are they? So it's ours as much as it's yours; all of ours, isn't it?

It's no different to the timber washed up here last year. We shared it, didn't we? Everyone shared it. That's worth a bit too, by the look of it. Never even seen a fish that big; and I've seen some big ones. 'S a monster of a fish. That horn's worth something too, I shouldn't wonder.'

'You can't, you can't kill her,' cried Daniel, appealing not to Big Tim now but to his friends. 'You can't let him do it. You heard what the Birdman said. It's all true, and I know him. He's a good man. He's not a spy like Big Tim says. Why should he lie? Can't you see he's trying to save us?'

But they were not listening, none of them were. They were staring out over the sea, a look of utter astonishment on every face. There was nothing there but the sound at first, a curious roaring and crying from the open sea beyond Popplestones that became a crescendo of thunderous snorting and whistling. Within minutes Popplestones was alive with whales. Great spouts of water shot into the air. Everywhere you looked in the bay shining black backs broke the surface, rocked a little and then rolled forward and vanished again under the water. All of Big Tim's friends had already fled up the beach, but he stayed with us as mesmerized as we were. Beside us, the stranded whale writhed and rolled in its grave of sand its tail thrashing in fury and frustration, its own whistling cry joining the chorus of the others out in Popplestones.

'They've come,' cried the Birdman. 'It's too late, too late!'

'What a catch!' shouted Big Tim. 'What a catch! There

must be dozens of them out there. Can't do it on our own though; we'll need help. I'm going back for help.' And he ran up the beach to join his friends. 'We're going, but we'll be back and we'll kill every one of them, Birdman.'

'What does he say?' the Birdman asked Daniel. 'I don't understand what he's saying. Is he going for help? I can't see what he's saying; he talks too fast for me. Is he going for help?'

'No,' said Daniel, 'He's going to fetch the whole island down here, but they won't be coming to help. They'll be coming to kill, Mr Woodcock, and we can't stop them. There'll be too many of them.'

'Not again,' said the Birdman. 'Oh please God, not again. We have to stop them, we have to stop them.'

11 LAST CHANCE

WE DID ALL WE COULD TO DISCOURAGE THE whales from coming in too close to the shore. Shouting and screaming at the water's edge, we hurled stones and driftwood at them but most fell far short and those few that did hit them did not seem to deter them. The Birdman's flock of gulls wheeled noisily overhead, but the whales took no notice of them either. All the time they were drifting closer and closer to the beach and disaster. Every faint whistle from the stranded whale seemed to drive the others out in the bay to distraction, sending them rolling and plunging in amongst each other and precipitating a chorus of thunderous snorting and whistling that subsided only when the whale lay still and silent again on the sand. But each furious flurry of activity left them that much nearer the shore and there seemed nothing we could do now to stop them beaching themselves.

'Gracie,' said the Birdman, 'you go back to the whale and try to keep her happy. Stroke her, Gracie. Talk to her, sing to her, anything so's she doesn't call out.' And he took off his sou'wester and handed it to me. 'It won't do to let her get too dry either, Gracie. You can use this for a bucket.'

So I went back and forth from the water's edge to the whale with the Birdman's sou'wester full of water. I began at her head, pouring the water all over her eyes and mouth. She seemed to relish it, blinking and rolling her head from side to side as the water ran down over her skin and into the sand, and all the while I talked to her quietly. I remember thinking as I looked into her eyes that she could understand me, that she could understand every word I said.

I was kneeling in the sand beside her head, stroking her behind the blowhole above her eyes, when I saw them coming back. They were hurrying along the path under Gweal Hill, Big Tim running out in front. It looked as if he had brought most of the island with him. Everyone had a weapon of some kind in his hand, a fork, an axe, a hoe or a scythe; and Daniel's father carried a harpoon over his shoulder. I looked for Mother amongst them but could not pick her out. The Vicar was there, his cassock tucked up into his trousers and Mr Wellbeloved was there too, striding out with his stick alongside Daniel's father.

'Stay where you are, Gracie,' the Birdman told me, 'and keep her quiet if you can.' By the time they reached the beach, the Birdman, Daniel and Prince stood between them and the stranded whale. No one spoke for a moment. They all stood looking incredulously at the Birdman and the whale, at Daniel and me, whispering anxiously amongst themselves. It was only when they noticed the rolling black backs breaking the water out in the bay that they began to talk aloud.

'See,' Big Tim shouted in triumph, pointing his machete. 'Didn't I tell you? Didn't I tell you? There's dozens of them out there. I said there was.'

'It's a narwhal,' said Mr Wellbeloved. 'Yes, I do believe it's a narwhal. Well I never. Only the males have tusks, you know. He's a long way from home. That's the kind of whale that the Eskimos hunt off Greenland. Quite what he's doing here I cannot imagine. If I might take a closer look . . .' As he stepped towards us Prince began to growl, his lip curling back above his teeth, his neck tense with fury. Mr Wellbeloved stopped where he stood.

'Look here, Mr Woodcock,' Daniel's father said, taking Mr Wellbeloved's arm and pulling him back, 'we don't much care what this thing is. Whale, narwhal, it doesn't matter to us. All that matters is that there's meat on it and ivory too by the look of it. That's money to us, Mr Woodcock. Anything washed up on our beaches is ours by right, always has been, Mr Woodcock; you know that.' The Birdman said nothing but looked along the ranks of islanders that faced him. 'And as for you, Daniel Pender,' Daniel's father went on, pointing at Daniel, 'you can come right back over here, else I'll take a strap to you right here and now in front of all these people. You've no business to be here with this man. You've been told time and time again.' Daniel stayed where he was alongside the Birdman.

'You can strap me all you want, Father,' he said, 'but you got to listen to Mr Woodcock. You got to listen to him. If you don't, then we're done for, all of us. You got to do what he says, Father.'

'Mr Woodcock,' Daniel's father said, his patience fast vanishing, 'are you going to move that dog or am I? Now I don't want anyone to get hurt . . .'

'He can't hear you, Father,' Daniel said. 'He's deaf. Gracie and me, we're the only ones he can understand.'

'Deaf?' said Daniel's father, and he was clearly taken aback. 'All right then, you tell him for us, Daniel. You tell him that the whale belongs to all of us and we aim to kill it and those out there in Popplestones as well. They're ours by right and he can't stop us. Tell him to stand aside.'

Daniel interpreted quietly and the Birdman nodded his understanding, putting his hand on Daniel's shoulder. He straightened up and faced Daniel's father. 'Then you will have to kill me first,' he said. 'This whale must go back to the sea where she belongs. Then we must drive them all back out to sea. If just one of them dies, the curse that fell on Samson when I was a boy will fall on you, and Bryher will be cursed forever. You must help me before it's too late.'

'Oh come on,' said Big Tim pushing his way through. 'We don't have to listen to this old fool. Those whales out there could turn round any minute and head back out to sea and we'd lose the lot of them.' And the crowd began to move slowly in towards us.

'Stand aside, Mr Woodcock,' said Daniel's father. 'You know we're within our rights. Out of the way now.' At once Prince was on his feet and the growl had turned to a snarl. Those just in front of him fell back, but the rest kept coming until we were almost surrounded. At that moment the whale must have sensed danger for she raised her head and whistled again, twisting and turning and thrashing the ground behind her. Popplestones Bay suddenly boiled with life.

'Don't do it, please Father,' cried Daniel backing down towards me. 'Don't do it. Listen to him. He's telling the truth. I know he is.' But I could see from the hardness in the faces around me that they were ignoring him, that they were no longer even listening as they closed in around us.

'Wait!' It was a voice from the back of the crowd, a voice I knew well. 'Wait!' Everyone looked round. They hushed instantly, and then stood to one side as my mother came forward, Aunty Mildred beside her. Mother looked first at me and then at the Birdman. 'You were up early this morning, Gracie,' she said. 'I wondered where you'd got to.'

'Had to go, Mother,' I said, standing up. 'I had to. Daniel came for me. Big Tim and all of them, they were going to attack the Birdman's cottage. Daniel heard them planning it, so we had to warn him, didn't we?'

'Were they indeed?' said Mother, looking around her. There was a hard edge to her voice I had never heard before. 'Did you know that, Mr Pender?' she asked, and Daniel's father looked hard at Big Tim.

'Well he deserved it,' said Big Tim. 'He was signalling to German submarines, I know he was. We seen him, didn't we?' But none of his friends supported him now.

Mother walked across to Big Tim and looked him in the eye. 'You know nothing, Tim Pender; because you don't think, you never have. You know only what you want to know. You're a bully and a coward and you should be ashamed of yourself.' And she turned and spoke to the crowd. 'This old man helped me and Gracie. He left honey and milk and bread on my doorstep when we needed it most. Just like you, I've known him all my life and never spoken to him, but in all that time I've never known him harm anyone. Yes, every one of us is frightened of him and we tell our children to keep out of his way; but what has he ever really done to harm any one of us?' There was silence. Mother came over to me and took me by the hand. 'I don't know what Gracie and Daniel have been up to, and I don't know why Mr Woodcock wants to save these creatures. I do know we owe it to him and to the two children at least to listen to them, to hear them out. If after that you still want to kill the whales, then you can. They'll still be here.' She did not wait for approval, she assumed it. She turned to Daniel. 'Tell us, Daniel. Tell us all about it.' And not a word was raised against her.

I wondered at the time that she was able to command such instant obedience. On reflection I think everyone was as shocked as I was at the sudden transformation in her. I certainly had never seen her so authoritative and passionate. All I know is that without a murmur, even from Big Tim, they all backed away and waited shamefaced for Daniel to begin.

Daniel turned to Mr Woodcock. 'Shall I tell them?' he asked, and the old man nodded.

'Tell them,' he said, 'tell them everything. But hurry, Daniel, hurry. There's no time to lose.'

They listened intently as Daniel told them of how the Birdman and his mother had witnessed the massacre of the whales on Samson all those years ago, how they had tried to stop it and failed, that it was the islanders' greed and cruelty that had brought the curse down on Samson. He told them the whole terrible story of the death of Samson, of the ghostship, of the starvation and disease that followed, of all the ships drawn to their destruction on the rocks off Samson, of the dogs the people had to eat to survive.

As the truth behind the age-old rumours came out, the islanders listened all the more closely. They heard how the people left one by one until finally the well had dried up and forced the Birdman and his mother off the island.

For some time no one said anything. They looked at each other uneasily, and then it was Big Tim that spoke up. 'So what? We don't know that any of it's true, do we? He could be making it all up, couldn't he? Where's the proof?'

'The proof's on Samson,' Daniel said. 'I've seen it – and Gracie's seen it too. We've seen the horn, haven't we, Gracie? In Mr Woodcock's cottage on Samson it was, hanging above the stove. Just like that one it is,' he said, pointing at the whale.

'You been over there, Gracie?' Mother asked me. 'You been over to Samson?'

'We couldn't help it, Mother,' I said. 'It was that night we went out fishing and the fog came down. Never told you before 'cos I knew you'd be angry. Didn't know where we were, Mother, honest. Couldn't see a thing. Then we saw this light and rowed towards it. We thought it was Bryher at first, but it turned out it was the Birdman's fire on Samson. He lights a fire on Samson whenever there's bad weather. It's to keep the ships away from the rocks.'

Suddenly Mother was beside me. Hands on hips, she faced the crowd. 'Well?' she said. 'What are you waiting for? If we don't hurry, every one of those whales will be on the beach and then we'll never be able to get them off. We need a sail to roll her onto and we need ropes. We'll need a horse, or a donkey, both maybe to haul her back into the sea. Hurry now.' This time there were no arguments. On the contrary there was a sudden stir of excitement. Somehow, Mother had galvanised the whole island into action. The Vicar and Aunty Mildred organised every spare man, woman and child into an extended line at the water's edge. There must have been a hundred people there advancing into the sea to keep the whales from coming in. Waist high in the water they were whistling and shouting and splashing, whilst behind them the rescue began.

It was Daniel's father who directed the delicate task of engineering the stranded whale back into the sea. 'Got to launch her gently, just like she was a boat,' he said. They dug a deep trench to one side of her and when the sail came they laid it in the bottom. Then they dug away the side of the ditch she was lying in and eased her sideways, rocking her gently until she slid down onto the sail. It took twelve men pushing, the Birdman, Mr Wellbeloved and Daniel's father amongst them, before the whale was finally in place.

All through the rescue I stayed by the whale's head whilst an endless relay of children with buckets, Big Tim and his friends mostly, fetched and carried water to keep the whale's skin wet. She was tiring quickly now. Her flourishes were less and less frequent and she had fallen almost silent. She moved quietly from time to time, her tiny eyes often closing for minutes on end so that sometimes I thought she might be dead. A bucket of water poured gently over her head seemed to revive her, but each time it took longer. She would open her wedge-shaped mouth under the horn and allow the water to trickle in through her teeth. I talked to her all the while, reassuring her as well as I could that it would not be long now before she was back with her friends and out at sea again. I could feel her breath on my fingers as I stroked the top of her head around her blowhole. She was breathing less often now and more deeply, almost as if she were going to sleep. Or was she dying slowly?

Friend and another donkey were hitched up already to the sail. At first it looked as if they would not be strong enough for the task. Their feet sank deep into the sand as they pulled and the whale did not move. What the Birdman said into Friend's ear no one knows, but whatever it was was enough, for they were soon hauling the whale down across the wet sand towards the sea. There were a dozen men or more straining at the sail at each side, so that the whale was returned to the water cradled in a kind of hammock. I stood back and watched with the others as the waves washed over her and she gradually came back to life. On the Birdman's advice we left her there wallowing in the shallows for some time, giving her time to regain her strength, to feel her buoyancy. Then to our delight she began to heave and thrash again and she let out a long wailing whistle. That seemed enough to satisfy the Birdman and we gathered around her and pushed her through the water towards the others that lay waiting for her out in the bay. There was a flurry out in the middle when she joined them and much rolling and groaning and whistling, an exultant chorus of joy at their reunion. Then she became one of them, and I was never sure which she was after that.

I thought, as everyone thought, that the job was done then, that once reunited they would turn for the open sea; but for some reason they seemed reluctant to leave the bay in spite of all we did to frighten them away. Big Tim it was who suggested that banging on tin trays and corrugated iron might do the trick, so we children were all sent home to fetch back any bit of sheet metal we could find that would serve as a drum. It was a good idea and the first time we all thundered on our makeshift drums it seemed to have an effect, for they turned and swam away; but then they stopped at the mouth of the bay and turned back again setting up such a row of whistling, whooping and snorting so that you would almost have thought they were talking back to our drums. Far from driving them away, the drumming only seemed to interest them and excite them.

All day long the islanders sustained this frantic effort. Everyone took turns in the water now, for it was too cold to stay there long. Hot soup and bread were brought out to the beach and kept warm over a fire in one corner of the beach, so that a ready supply of food was on hand all day. We had one brief taste of success when a pair of the whales was spotted swimming out to sea, past Gweal Rock. However the others did not follow, so that by nightfall most of the whales were still trapped in Popplestones, unable or unwilling to find their way out.

The Birdman, Daniel and I were sitting drinking our soup by the fire when the Birdman had the idea. His face was ashen with cold and exhaustion, but suddenly there was an urgency in his voice. 'Look where they are,' he said, getting to his feet and pointing out into the bay. 'Look at them.' The whales were lying together in a pack in the dark waters on the far side of Popplestones. 'It's the fire,' he said. 'It's the fire. They're as far from the fire as they can be. They don't like fire.'

Flaming torches, oil lamps, piles of burning brushwood and driftwood, we used anything, anything that would burn. We lit fires all along the rocks around the bay; and then the Birdman, with a long line of islanders on either side of him waving their torches above their heads, waded out into the sea towards the whales. We children were told to stay on the beach. It was too dangerous now, out in the dark water with the whales' flailing tails and the sea whipped up into a frenzy by a fresh offshore wind. So we stayed and watched the line of torches as they moved out into the bay.

Only minutes later they brought the Birdman back, Daniel's father and the Vicar carrying him out of the sea. A wave had knocked the breath out of him, Daniel's father said as they laid him down by the fire beside us.

'I'll be all right,' the Birdman said, struggling onto his elbows. 'Let me get out there. We need everyone out there.'

'I think you've done enough, Mr Woodcock,' said the Vicar. 'They're going, they're turning. We can manage without you now. You nearly drowned out there. You stay here and rest.' And much against his will, he did. Mother put a blanket around him and Daniel and I huddled close to him, and Prince came to lie down at our feet. 'Maybe it'll be all right, children,' the Birdman said.

'Maybe it will be, after all.'

It was the line of flaming torches that at last made the whales leave for the open sea; for with a final flourish of triumphant whistling and snorting, and shooting great fountains into the air, they swam out past Gweal Island and left us in the gathering dark. A great cheer went up all around the bay, but beside us the Birdman was still not happy. He was on his feet again by now. He made everyone build beacons all along the beach to be sure they did not come back during the night; and even when almost everyone had left Popplestones for home he still would not go.

Mother asked him to come home with us. She begged him to come. 'Tell him it's a cold night, Daniel, and he can't sleep in a house with no windows. He's soaked to the skin. Tell him he must come home with us.'

Daniel told him and the Birdman smiled and shook his head. 'I'll be warm enough by the fire,' he said. 'I shall stay here and Prince will stay with me to keep me company, won't you, Prince? Maybe later when it gets light I'll take the boat out. I want to be sure they've gone – got to be sure they don't come back. You take those two children of mine home before they catch cold.' And as we were leaving, he called out without turning round. 'It's over now, children. The curse of Samson is redeemed, finished. All will be well now, I promise you. You'll see.'

So we left him there in the glow of the fire with Prince sitting beside him. As we went we saw the gulls settling on the beach all around him and from nowhere his one-legged kittiwake flew up and landed on his shoulder.

No one ever saw the Birdman again. They found his sou'wester washed up on Hell Bay some days later, but his boat was never found. I have always thought that he knew he might not be coming back because otherwise he would never have left Prince behind on the beach, and because of the remnants of a shell message we found the next morning in the sand beside the dog. The shells were scattered but we could still make out the letters 'Z.W.'.

12 THE END OF IT ALL

I HAD NEVER SEEN THE CHURCH SO FULL AS IT WAS that next Sunday morning, not even at Christmas. It was a service, the Vicar said, not just for one but for two fine men of Bryher who had given their lives for us all. I did not hear much of what he said. He had that kind of droning, dreary voice that is impossible to listen to for very long. I remember sitting in the front pew with Mother on one side of me and Daniel on the other, and feeling very important and not nearly as sad as I knew I should be. I prayed though, or I tried to; but it came out as a thought rather than a prayer in the end. I was thinking how good it would be if Father and the Birdman were to meet up in Heaven, and I wondered what they would say about me. Daniel sat hunched up in a stiff collar beside me, his hair unnaturally slicked down. On the way home afterwards we walked along together. Daniel was angry.

'They still don't trust him,' he said. 'After all he's done for them, they still don't believe him. Father told me to keep off Samson. Says he wants to be sure the curse is finished. He says only time will tell. He's still scared, Gracie. They're all scared, except Aunty Mildred. She's not scared of anything. Only one way to prove it to them, Gracie. We'll have to go and fetch that horn back. If they see that they'll have to believe everything then, won't they? Even Father, even Big Tim.'

But for two weeks after the memorial service the winter gales came and lashed the islands and not a boat could move out of Bryher. It was too dangerous even to cross the sheltered channel to Tresco. That meant there was no school and I was grateful for that. We had brought Prince back to live with us in Southill Cottage, and those horrible goats came too, much to my disgust. Mother said someone had to look after them. I wanted Daniel to look after them, but Daniel's father would not have any animals near his house, and so I found myself milking them twice a day. We had to leave the Birdman's hens and Friend up on Heathy Hill, not because we wanted to but because we could not catch them. Each day during the gales Daniel and I went up there to feed them, hoping to be able to catch them and bring them home; but they were always too wily for us, even when they were hungry.

Then one morning we woke up and the wind had died; the tamarisk tree outside my window was still at last. I lay there beside Mother hoping the sea would be too restless after the storm for us to go to school that day. I did think it was strange when the church bell began to ring, for by my reckoning it was a Monday morning; but I was quite content to believe that I was wrong and that I had another day without school. So I lay back on my pillow and was almost asleep again when Mother sat up suddenly.

'It's not Sunday,' she said. 'The church bell's ringing and it's not Sunday.'

'You sure it isn't Sunday?' I asked. 'It could be, couldn't it?'

'It's Monday, Gracie,' Mother said, 'and a fine day by the look of it, and you're going to school. Out of bed with you.'

'Then why are they ringing the bell if it's Monday?' I asked.

'No idea, but whatever it is it can wait until after breakfast.' Mother climbed out of bed. 'Come on now, Gracie, hurry else you'll miss the school boat.' She looked across the bed at me. 'And just so you won't miss that boat I'll walk you down to the quay; we can find out then why they're ringing that bell.'

Prince came with us sniffing every gateway as they passed, his tail constantly circling, and all the while as we walked up the path the bell kept ringing and ringing. Daniel was not waiting for me as he usually was and every house as we passed seemed to be empty, the front doors flung open wide and left there. The bell had stopped ringing by the time we reached Aunty Mildred's house. We were just passing her gate when we first heard the crowd. As we rounded the bend we saw the quay below us was full of people. You could not see the quay for the crowd. The school boat was there but no one was getting into it. There was another boat beside it, one that often came from St Mary's. Everyone was laughing and clapping and cheering. And then one of them, a man in blue it was, was hoisted on their shoulders and they began to march in a great calvalcade up the path towards us. Prince sat down as he often did when he needed time to consider things.

'Who's that, Gracie?' Mother said, her eyes squinting into the sun. 'What's all the fuss about?'

Daniel was haring up the path towards us and shouting at us as he came. 'That'll show them, Gracie, that'll show them. Now they'll have to believe us. It's over, just like he promised. The curse of Samson is over. Can't you see who it is, Gracie, can't you see?'

And now I could see. Mother saw too, but she could not believe her eyes. As they set my father down on his feet again one of them handed him a stick and the crowd fell silent around him. He looked at Mother, then took off his sailor's cap. 'Bit late for breakfast, am I, Clemmie?' Mother stared at him. 'Well don't look at me like that. It's me, Clemmie, honest it is. They tell me I'm supposed to be dead and drowned, but I'm not. Didn't they tell you I was coming? No, by the look on your face I don't think they can have done. What do I have to do to prove it to you? Here, take my hand, Clemmie, feel that. It's me isn't it? Tell me it's me or I'll begin to doubt it myself. I had my ship sunk from under me, Clemmie – torpedoed off Gallipoli she was, went down in two minutes. There was no one else left alive in the water except me. I hung on to a bit of a lifeboat for a whole day and night and then a fishing boat picked me up. You can't believe it, can you? Well neither could I, I can tell you. I'm a lucky fellow, Clemmie. I don't deserve to be here, but I am. I've got sick leave. Knocked my leg about a bit when I fell in the water, but I won't be needing this old stick for too long.' Father looked down at me. 'Ride home, Gracie?' he said. 'Just off to school, were you? Well Mr Wellbeloved will have to do without you for a day, won't he? Hop up,' he said crouching down, and I jumped up onto his shoulders. 'Coming, Clemmie?' he said and took her hand. 'I could eat a horse.'

That same afternoon every boat on Bryher set out over a sun-dancing sea for Samson. No one stayed behind, not even Big Tim. Mind you, I did notice he was the last one to set foot on Samson when we got there.

They marvelled at the horn above the fireplace in the cottage – and everyone wanted to touch it just to be sure it was not made of wood. We roamed the island from end to end. The great black rabbits were everywhere and Prince chased them ineffectually all afternoon. He rampaged over the island like a wild thing and I found him stretched out on the bed in the Birdman's cottage, his tongue lolling out of his mouth and dripping.

'He's thirsty,' I said. 'Needs a drink.'

'There'll be water in the well now,' said Daniel. 'I know there will be; there has to be.' And we ran down the hillside together, Prince bounding along after us. Sure enough the well was full, full to the brim. We all three lay down on the ground, put our faces in it and drank together.

Everyone drank from the well on Samson that day as if it were the elixir of life, and after that no one ever doubted the Birdman's story, not in my hearing anyway.

* * *

If you ever do go to the Isles of Scilly, go over to Samson and look round for yourself. The old ruined cottages are still there, a mound of limpet shells outside each one; and you'll find the well full of water. No one lives there, so you'll have only the terns and the black rabbits for company. You'll be quite alone.

MORE BRILLIANT TITLES
FROM AWARD-WINNING AUTHOR,
MICHAEL MORPURGO:

KING OF THE CLOUD FORESTS

The creature was crouched by the fire and when he rose his bulk filled the room. He was like a giant man but yet not a man . . .

It's 1941. Escaping from China as the Japanese invade, Ashley and Uncle Sung embark on a dangerous journey across the Himalayas towards India.

Then Ashley finds himself alone in the hostile mountains, battling for life. He is just about to give up all hope, when he has a mysterious and terrifying encounter . . .

Kensuke's Kingdom

MICHAEL MORPURGO

WINNER OF THE CHILDREN'S BOOK AWARD 2000

RECOMMENDED SUPER READ FOR
WORLD BOOK DAY 2001

'I heard the wind above me in the sails. I remember thinking, this is silly, you haven't got your safety harness on, you haven't got your lifejacket on. You shouldn't be doing this. Then the boat veered violently and I was thrown sideways. I had no time to grab the guard-rail. I was in the cold of the sea before I could even open my mouth to scream'

Washed up on an island in the Pacific, Michael struggles to survive on his own. He can't find food, he can't find water. In the end, he curls up to die. When he wakes, there is a plate beside him of fish, of fruit, and a bowl of fresh water. He is not alone . . .

'A magnificent contemporary odyssey: a beautifully-written account of a boy's voyage of discovery' *TES*

'Exciting and thought-provoking' *Observer*

'This is a wonderful book, a modern day Robinson Crusoe and is simply too good to miss' Wendy Cooling

The Wreck of Zanzibar

MICHAEL MORPURGO

WINNER OF THE BEEFEATER CHILDREN'S
NOVEL AWARD

When the General Lee runs aground, Laura is the one to spot her; and then the race is on – can Bryher's gig beat the boat from St Mary's – and win the chance to repair the wrecked ship, securing work and money for her tiny community?

It's 1907 and life on the Scilly Isles is bleak and difficult. But then a violent storm brings an unexpected harvest to the island . . .

An exciting and absorbing story of adventure and survival.